Night and Day

A Gideon Lowry Mystery

by John Leslie

Copyright Info

The author would like to thank Tom Corcoran and Marilyn Shames for their assistance in creating and proofreading this edition.

Cover photograph © 2013 Tom Corcoran

CreateSpace Edition

Please visit www.JohnLeslieAuthor.com

Night and Day

1.

A handful of people sat around the piano bar in the Pier House soaking up wine and air-conditioning. It was early evening in mid-July. A florid-faced man with a diamond ring that was too small for his pudgy finger kept thumping the ring against the lid of the baby grand, his other hand around the waist of a skittish blonde who had had just enough to drink to loosen up her vocal chords. She didn't know many of the words to the tune I was playing, but she hummed to the syncopated rhythm and would then really belt it when a familiar phrase came her way. "Listen to the *hmm hmm* of the cottonwood trees...," she sang. "Don't fence me in." The florid-faced guy banging his ring on the piano pulled her against him.

When it was over, there was some listless applause as I stood up and walked over to the bar where Ronnie had a club soda ready for me. "Rowdy crowd," I said.

Ronnie grinned. "Don't complain. It's work."

She was right. Ronnie had worked the bar at a Duval Street hotel where I played weekend gigs last winter. When business fell off there in the spring, I was laid off and Ronnie had moved here, a resort hotel on Key West's harbor where there was always a little more action during the slower summer months. Ronnie had suggested bringing me in to replace Bobby Nesbitt, who was gone for the summer. I was now working four nights a week. GIDEON LOWRY AT THE PIANO. Serving up Irving Berlin, George Gershwin, and Cole Porter.

I looked at my watch. It was eight-thirty, the dinner hour. I went to pee, and when I came out of the rest room, only three people remained as I made my way back to the piano. The piano thumper had left with his squeeze. I sat down, struck a couple of chords, running through my mental list of tunes, then someone touched my shoulder and said, "Mr. Lowry?"

I looked up. A woman wearing a beret and sunglasses, her lips the color of a plum, stood beside the piano.

"Gideon," I said, continuing to play soft chords. "What can I do for you?"

"You're the private detective?" Her voice was faintly husky, a certain breathless quality to it. I liked it.

I said I was.

"I'd like to make an appointment with you."

"No problem." People hadn't exactly been beating the door down for my services recently. "Tomorrow morning soon enough?"

The woman inclined her head. I couldn't see her eyes. She seemed nervous, though, and young, standing there gripping the edge of the piano. A kind of charged force surrounded her, I thought, like the distant, mysterious hum along a power line. "Is nine o'clock too early?"

"I can be there then."

"You know where my office is?"

She nodded. She wore a tunic top with a clerical-style collar and black tights. Trim.

On some impulse I changed keys, striking an E-flat chord, and softly began to play "Night and Day." The woman in the beret started to turn away, then cocked her head to one side, listening.

"What's your name?"

She didn't seem to hear me. Or if she did, she was ignoring me. A microphone rested inside the piano, and she reached in and picked it out, and tapping her hand against her thigh, she began to sing. "You are the one." She turned it into a torch song. There was a hush in the bar as the three people who remained turned their attention to this temptress who was dragging the notes of the song up and down over hot coals with all the yearning and burning inside of her, holding the final note in an uneven tremolo. When she was done, no one moved. Her spell was cast. She dropped the mike back in its place, touched a finger to her lips, and walked out. I stood up and went to the bar. "Who was that?" I asked Ronnie.

"You don't know Asia?"

"Asia who?"

"Just Asia. Like Madonna, no last name. I wouldn't have recognized her until she sang. What a voice! Can you believe she just walked in here like that?"

I went back to the piano and played my heart out, but it wasn't the same. The music had gone out the door with a scamp of a girl in a black beret.

At two o'clock in the morning I made my way home by bicycle along the shadowy streets, the smell of stale beer from the downtown bars mingling with the heady aroma of flowering frangipani. Home was the upper end of Duval Street. Main Street. The raucous, rowdy carnivallike strip of bars and T-shirt shops and food emporiums where tourists prowled endlessly and whose face changed to satisfy every passing fad. I was an anachronism, a dinosaur on a street of dreams that stretched thinly between the Gulf of Mexico and the Atlantic Ocean.

Chaining the bike to the front porch, I went inside, fixed myself a ham sandwich, and carried it and a glass of milk back into the front office, where I sat at the desk eating and looking out the window, trying to decide whether I should have the peeling gold letters advertising LOWRY INVESTIGATIVE SERVICES on the windows on either side of the door repainted.

Tom, the neutered cat that slept in the lower-right desk drawer, got up and jumped out, making a sound like a soft drum roll as his feet hit the hardwood floor. He arched his back, yawned, and looked up at me before stretching out on the floor, belly up, beneath the languid turning of the overhead paddle fan, which shifted the damp air.

Night and Day

Across the street, the red and blue pennants hanging around the perimeter of the used-car lot were limp in the breezeless air, their glossy surfaces glinting like diamonds from the reflected light of the streetlamps. I finished the sandwich and opened the top desk drawer and searched with my hand until it closed over the steel of the gun that lived in the drawer. This had become a nightly ritual, a ceremony as fastidiously conducted as an exorcism.

The gun was a .45-caliber Colt with white bone grips that were turning yellow. It was similar to the sidearm General George S. Patton was famous for carrying. Patton was the kind of man my father, Captain Billy Lowry III, most admired. Captain Billy had bought the gun sometime in the 1940s. He bought it to kill sharks on his charter fishing boat, the *Low Blow*. In 1958 he used it to kill himself. And nearly thirty-five years later my brother, Carl Lowry, the state senator from Key West, had used this same weapon to take his own life. Much of my family history seemed tied to this gun, and that history was, from my point of view, self-inflicted.

I looked at the ancient pendulum clock on the wall, another part of my inheritance from the Lowry family. Time and death. It was almost three o'clock in the morning. I stood up and straightened the sepia-toned photographs of my mother and father, which always hung slightly askew on the wall behind the desk. Tom got up and followed me into the kitchen. I opened the refrigerator and took out some mullet I'd picked up earlier in the day from the charter-boat area, brought home, and cooked. I tore off a chunk of its white flesh and placed it in his food bowl on the floor by the back door. When I stood up, I glanced quickly out the glass in the back door to the motel that was nearing completion. I'd waged a war against its construction, and lost. Now, unless I moved, I was doomed for the rest of my life to a view of gray concrete rising up two stories little more than fifty feet from my back porch.

I went back into the office and pushed the gun into the recesses of my desk drawer where, despite my efforts to the contrary, I couldn't forget it, as if it could shed clues to my future the way it had so clearly defined my past. We were in for another long, hot tropical summer.

I laced my fingers behind my head and leaned back in the chair, watching the moonlight spread across the sky. I thought of an etherized patient and the poetry of T. S. Eliot, which had stuck with me, a gift from my mother, Phyllis. I can still hear her reading, as she did so often when my brother, Carl, and I were growing up.

I looked down at the hem of my khakis where, yes, there were now cuffs. I smiled. Growing old. At fifty-seven I was indeed wearing the bottoms of my trousers rolled. Phyllis would have been amused.

It had been a while since I had taken a drink. And the last woman with whom I'd been intimate had left Key West, moving to Miami. Casey and I had not seen each other, although she had promised not to be a stranger.

I considered eating a peach and wearing white flannel trousers as I walked along the beach with the mermaids singing each to each, but no longer, I guessed, to me.

Nevertheless, I have kept my ear to the conch shell, that hard, glistening mollusk that has provided not only a symbol for my people, but also our nickname. Patience is an asset we Conchs understand, an asset inherent in all people who live surrounded by water. I grow old, but I continue to listen for the mermaid's song.

2.

At seven-thirty the next morning, Friday, I walked three blocks over to the drugstore for breakfast. I liked this hour of the day with its small-town tranquility, when the few people around were other locals getting an early start before the town was taken over by tourists. I grabbed a paper and sat at the counter, nodding to several of my fellow citizens, among whom was Sweetwater, who sat opposite me at the counter. In all the years I'd been coming here I was certain I could count on both hands the number of times Sweets had been absent from this morning ritual.

The twin U-shaped counters were filled with guys in jeans and T-shirts, construction workers, and crews for City Electric, who jousted with the pair of waitresses in their white aprons bustling between the counters with coffeepots and breakfast platters; both of these women had been working here for more years than I cared to remember.

I doctored the coffee that Yolanda put in front of me, gave her my order, and turned to the Keys section of the Miami paper to see what had befallen my people the past twenty-four hours. We were in the midst of another celebration, Hemingway Days. Another festival to attract the hardy souls who could withstand the withering summer while celebrating our most famous tourist attraction's birthday. Days and nights of drinking and partying while burly, gray-bearded men sought to win a competition for resemblance to the writer who had lived here for a decade in the 1930s.

Other news was of a rally being held in protest against the

possibility of oil drilling off the Keys' coast. A few oil companies had purchased leases from the state, held them for several years, with the leases now up for renewal. The protesters wanted a permanent ban against any offshore drilling, arguing that it would mean devastation to the economy and our natural resources in the event of an oil spill. For once my people seemed to have found themselves in agreement on an environmental matter.

There were those who had resisted the efforts of newcomers, whose general purpose in life seemed to be to save us from ourselves, by recognizing that time and the tides would erode some of our saviors' impatience. I smiled, thinking of Captain Billy, when I read that the Chamber of Commerce, our city fathers, and the environmentalists were all of an accord.

Captain Billy had had no time for rules and regulations. He was of a time and place where independence belonged to those who carried the fattest wallets and the biggest *cojónes,* a combination he highly approved. My mother, Phyllis, I believe, saw this for what it was: bluster. Which couldn't have made it any more appealing to her, but since she, too, was of that same time, though her place was adopted, she put up with the captain's swagger, probably because she recognized that he was harmless—to all, that is, except himself.

One of my mother's favorite expressions came back to me now in the pages of the paper. Oil and water do not mix. It was the protester's creed, literally, while Phyllis had used it as a figure of speech to describe the disparity that existed in her life; mostly, I'm now sure, as reflected by her union with Captain Billy.

My brother, Carl, the senator, had early on aligned his political fortunes with those who followed Captain Billy's strongman philosophy—of course in this place at that time there was no other. The irony, however, is that Carl, after over thirty years in the Florida legislature, discovered the environment only a short time before his death, but insured that he would be remembered forever for that late conversion.

I finished the article and then noticed a small column at the bottom of the page announcing that Asia had arrived in town. Asia, nothing more. Which is how I learned she was a recording artist who had apparently come to Key West in search of a house. I was not only a dinosaur but it also seemed I'd been culturally deprived in my life down here, since before she'd walked in the bar where I was playing last night, I'd never heard of Asia.

The rest of the news was wearying, the continuing saga of control for the almighty tourist dollar. It seemed we had been ruined, turned into a town of grasping, warring relatives for the sake of strangers' money.

I turned to the sports section and ate my breakfast. When I'd finished and was dawdling over a third cup of coffee, Sweetwater came over and sat on the empty stool next to me.

"How do, Bud," he said, his voice as tinted as his black skin.

"No complaints." My first wife, Peggy, had given me the nickname Bud when we were in high school and it had stuck. "How goes it with you, Sweets?"

"Got myself a new job." Many years ago Sweetwater had worked with my father at City Electric, and Captain Billy had, on occasion, taken him out on the *Low Blow* as a mate. Before the advent of electronics Sweetwater was famous for his ability to find fish in our nearby waters.

I thought of Sweets as being in retirement now. "What kind of a job?"

"Going to referee the boxing matches over at the Hemin'way House."

I shook my head. The boxing matches were part of the Hemingway Days festivities. Sweetwater was pushing eighty, though his body still suggested the strength and grace of a prizefighter. A faded rose tattoo flowered across the muscled biceps of his right arm. As a young man he had once sparred with Hemingway when the writer was living here in the thirties. But I remembered most Sweets's baritone voice booming across the neighborhood from the black church near our home on William Street when I was growing up. And more recently I remember him escorting my brother to his grave just as he had escorted my father in 1958. In my head I could hear the slow cadence of the bass drum Sweetwater played.

Now it appeared that one of those warring relatives in the city had found a way to capture more tourist money, by putting Sweetwater on display, using him to create more Hemingway myth. With Sweetwater, however, they were getting the real thing, no myth. Still, it saddened me.

"Why are you doing this?"

"I can use the money, Bud." Sweets grinned. "They paying me fifty bucks. Be in that ring every night they want me."

"What did Hemingway pay you to spar with him?"

"Fifty cents, sometimes a buck if he was feelin' generous, you know."

"But that was sixty years ago."

"Like it was yesterday. Still feel the leather of that man's glove poppin' me in the face."

I finished my coffee. "Who's fighting?"

"Couple of local youngsters. They buildin' up to a main event for the end of the week and Papa's birthday with some kids down from Miami."

"You need any help, Sweets, I've got a little money saved." After the probate court finished with my brother's estate, I was suddenly fifty thousand dollars richer.

Sweetwater stood up, all six feet two inches of him, still arrow straight. He grinned through crooked and missing teeth. "Naw, I can still make a living. I 'member your daddy always loved a good fight."

"Don't sell out to the bastards."

"No way," Sweets replied, and walked to the door.

I watched him leave, another dinosaur in a town where tourism was king and compromise the queen. It was an insult for a man of Sweetwater's age and dignity to be subjected to such fealty.

Yes, Captain Billy loved the fights. He was a working-class man with not a few prejudices. His life was one of boastful pride in his identity with his background, coupled with an unstated desire to be more than the working-class stiff that he was. Phyllis, I suppose, fulfilled that desire to some extent in the early days of their marriage before resentment set in and my father realized their differences were set in ways that were not to be changed by mere desire, and he became embittered.

In a way, my brother and I represented the two sides of Captain Billy's nature. I was the workingman, toiling for years as a cop and a fisherman before going into business for myself. My brother, Carl, was educated and sophisticated, having been a member of the state's political elite throughout his life. Perhaps it wasn't quite that simple, but looking back on it, I thought I could see my father's manipulative hand at work.

The corporate world, the world of high finance and politics, was a mystery to me. And to the extent that I had an appreciation for the arts, I owed my mother, but I was no more comfortable in that world than I could imagine Captain Billy would have been.

It was eight-thirty when I finished my coffee and walked home to the possibility of my first job in more than a week, with Asia's voice still vivid in my mind.

3.

Since Carl's death, work had been difficult. Not only because of the emotional toll that the death of my last immediate family member had taken, but also because I had jeopardized my main source of income—work for the state attorney's office—by an investigation of my own into the internal affairs of that office, an investigation that had resulted in the resignation of one of their attorneys. Since then I'd become a kind of pariah for the head of that office, and work ground to a halt.

Instead of looking for state witnesses or taking depositions, I was cooling my heels in my own office, waiting for the phone to ring or the door to open. It had been a period of adjustment, a time for some personal reflection, time that I probably needed. Now, however, work seemed my only refuge.

There had been a few odd jobs, of course—recovering a parrot stolen by a guy who'd been jilted by his girlfriend, and investigating the disappearance of a fifteen-year-old runaway. I found her, living with a shrimper on Stock Island. She had not been shanghaied, but nevertheless she seemed relieved to be found, happy to go home after two weeks bouncing around on a shrimp boat twenty miles offshore. Day after day she'd been put to work heading shrimp under the hot sun, after nights of listening to the creak and clang of the boat as its nets were dragged over the seafloor in search of the elusive pink bugs.

For me, these jobs paid too few bills, and despite a fat bank account due to the largesse of my brother, I needed to work. Needed it emotionally and physically, as much to get away

11

from myself and my dark thoughts as for any monetary needs. At one time the bottle had taken care of that escape route, but I hoped I had kicked that habit for good.

Asia came in at a few minutes past nine. Gone was the beret; her dark hair, with a streak of silver fetchingly highlighted along one side, was pulled back from her face. When she removed her sunglasses, I could see her face was stark and severe, exaggerated further by dark eyeliner around her black eyes and the reddest of lipsticks covering full lips. She wore jeans and a white blouse, her feet in thin-strapped leather sandals, the paint on her toes matching that on her lips.

She held out a thin, manicured hand, the flesh soft and slightly cool to the touch. The sunglasses dangled from a leather cord around her neck. For a moment I worried about not having air-conditioning, despite what I considered was a moderate temperature. It probably hadn't broken eighty, but I became uncomfortable with the idea of her sweating. She could have been a model, an actress. She had the cool, distant looks of someone accustomed to being recognized. We got our share of those people in Key West.

"You remember me," she said, a hint of a smile.

"How could I forget?" I turned on the overhead fan, the paddles groaning under the weight of dust, and gestured to the wicker chair in front of my desk.

She sat down, crossed her legs, and took a cigarette from a small leather purse she'd been carrying in her hand. I emptied an ashtray and pushed it across the desk before sitting down in my swivel chair.

"You didn't know me last night, did you?"

I may have blushed. "Nope. Never heard of you until last night."

"I just never know. Sometimes people have preconceived ideas." She drew on the cigarette, which she then stubbed out in the ashtray only half-smoked. "I shouldn't be smoking these," she said, mostly, it seemed, to herself.

"A nasty habit." I'd given the things up years ago.

She shook her head petulantly. "My voice."

I nodded. That, too.

A thin smile parted her lips for a moment. It annoyed me. I felt as if I were being toyed with and it made me irritable. I was not particularly well tuned to popular culture, mostly because I'd spent my life down here at the end of the road. I had no TV, read the papers mainly for local and sports news, and generally let the world go round on its own wobbly and, as far as I was concerned, misguided course.

"Shall we start over?" I asked, reminding myself that I needed work. "Tell me about yourself."

"I'm a singer. Some records. And MTV."

I shook my head. "MTV?"

She looked at me as if I were an alien, disbelief written across her face. For a moment I thought she was angry, then she laughed, raised a hand to her face, and really laughed. I felt better, glad to know that she had it in her.

"You've never heard of MTV?" The eyeliner began to run as tears streaked her eyes. "You got a tissue?"

I got up and walked back to the bathroom and brought out a box of Kleenex. When I got back, she had it under control. She dabbed at her eyes with the Kleenex and managed to look just as good, maybe better without the coloring pencil.

"Oh, that's grand. Just grand."

I'd never before heard a woman use the word grand in that way. It intrigued me. "Asia, what is it I can do for you?"

"Find my husband."

"Who is he?"

"Frank Maguire."

"Should I know him?"

"Not a chance," Asia said, lighting another cigarette.

4.

According to Asia, Frank Maguire was a writer. A guy from L.A.—Asia said "LaLa Land"—who wrote for newspapers and magazines out there.

"A journalist?" I asked.

Well, no, Frank didn't like to think of himself as a journalist. He wanted to write novels, had in fact been working on a novel for several years. A few years ago he'd also written a book about Ernest Hemingway in Hollywood.

"A biography?"

Well, no, not exactly, Asia said. It was sort of a mixture of fact and fiction.

I shrugged, feeling further removed from popular culture. I'd never heard of MTV, and here was one of its stars looking for her husband, who wrote books that were neither fact nor fiction.

While she talked, Asia continued to smoke her Benson & Hedges Lights, taking a couple of drags before snubbing one out and a few seconds later lighting another. There was something about her, some appeal, and I thought I was beginning to understand it. Despite whatever fame she might have had, Asia reminded me of a stray, a waif. And I reminded myself that it could have been calculated on her part and that I was old enough to be her father.

"When did you last see him?" I asked.

"Oh, I don't know, a year ago maybe."

One year ago. "And you're just now looking for him?"

"Well, we've been estranged."

Huh-uh. Very strange. "Have you tried calling him?" I asked, not without sarcasm.

"Gideon, please. It's complicated."

No doubt. "Tell me about it."

She had married Frank Maguire a couple of years after he had published his book on Hemingway, Asia told me. At the time she was just breaking into the music business. Originally from New York, she had gone out to LaLa Land when she was nineteen, worked in some clubs there, met a few people in the business—she always referred to it as the "business"—back when MTV was just in bloom. She'd gotten a couple of breaks over the next couple of years, and the rest, she said, was history.

I was beginning to get the picture. "You were married to Frank, becoming a star, and his career was going nowhere."

Asia was young, probably in her mid-twenties, and despite the sophistication and worldly attitude, I detected a scared girl.

Asia allowed a brief smile. "Something like that."

"When was the last time you talked to him?"

"A few months ago. Maybe less."

"About?"

Frank needed money. He'd called her once before to borrow money but without ever paying any of it back. He was desperate, he told her, and on the verge of a big break. He needed some backing to finish a project he was working on. Since that time Asia had never heard from him again. She had tried in the past couple of months to reach him, but his phone had been disconnected, and there was no forwarding address for him. The few people they still knew in common had no idea where Frank was. He wasn't publishing in the papers in California, and the publications he had written for had no information about him.

Frank Maguire had vanished.

"And that's a problem for you because..."

"Because I want a divorce."

15

"Why? You've been separated for a long time, living apart, why now?"

Asia lit another cigarette. "I'm afraid," she said through a cloud of smoke.

"Of Frank?"

Asia shook her head. "Frank is ten years older than I am, and I was too young when we got married. We had a lot of ambition and things just sort of clicked for me... but we had agreed to help each other if one of us made it."

"A written agreement?"

"No, nothing like that. It's just that I knew after about a year of being married that it wasn't right."

"What wasn't right?"

"The marriage." She looked away as if she'd heard someone behind her, but apart from the two us the room was empty. "Besides, I wasn't exactly... well, faithful."

"It happens." An image of this girl—I could hardly think of her as a woman—flashed across my mind. She was much too young for me and yet she stirred excitement, the kind of excitement that would lead to nothing but trouble. Which annoyed me even further. "Why didn't you get divorced when you separated?"

"Frank didn't want to, and I didn't really care at the time."

"He thought you might get back together?"

"Maybe, I don't really know. It was sometimes hard to know what Frank thought."

"And now you're afraid he's going to come after you for money. Is that it?"

"I want to divorce him, and I'm willing even to offer him a settlement."

"How much of a settlement?"

"Fifty grand." It didn't sound anything like the way she'd said *grand* earlier.

"That seems generous." Suddenly Asia didn't seem quite so young; or so vulnerable.

"I think so."

"But you think Frank might not be satisfied."

"I have a major contract coming up for a new recording. It's a lot of money. I'm trying to protect myself."

I thought I saw a patina of sweat above her upper lip, and the white blouse she wore was beginning to lose some of its starch. "Why have you come to Key West?"

"I think Frank is here."

"Why?"

"He had an obsession with Hemingway. He had often talked about coming here, getting out of L.A."

"But why so furtively?"

"You'll have to ask Frank. It's the way he is."

"Assuming I go to work for you."

"How much do you get paid?"

"A hundred and fifty a day plus expenses."

Asia opened her slim bag and brought out some money. I watched as she counted out ten crisp, new hundred-dollar bills. She pushed them all across the desk to me.

"Will that get you started?"

"With pleasure."

5.

At ten o'clock I biked over to the library on Fleming Street. I found Mary, the preservationist of local lore, at her desk in the reference department. The Keys Archives. Mary and I went to school here, after which she dedicated her life to keeping the history of these islands intact. In the process came an addiction to cigarettes, which left her with scarred lungs and suffering from chronic asthma.

"Bud Lowry," Mary wheezed. "I'm glad to see you."

I couldn't imagine why. Mary had a reputation for being less than sociable, sometimes even ferocious when pestered by the public. She liked cataloging and filing and rummaging through yellowing papers, at home amidst the clutter of our people's past lives, less so when dealing with ones in the present. I had not seen Mary since she'd provided me with background material for my investigation into a matter of history that caused my brother to take his life—a matter that would never be registered in Mary's tabulation of our history.

"I've been putting together a file on Carl. I wonder if you have anything you want to contribute."

A brother I'd never known until the last days of his life. "I don't think so. All of Carl's papers were left in his home here and given to the city."

"Yes, I know that," Mary said rather testily. "I thought you might have something from the family. Some memento."

Sadly, I thought of the gun that lay in my desk drawer. That and a photo or two and the clock were about all I had kept of any family heirlooms. I shook my head. "I don't keep that kind

18

of stuff."

Mary looked at me as if I had three eyes, then waved a hand in front of her face. "Bud, I can't believe you. These things are important."

"For who?"

"Oh, you're hopeless, Bud Lowry. What are you doing in here anyway?"

"Looking for a writer."

"What, do you think they live here? We keep books, not their authors."

"This guy wrote a biography of Hemingway." Among other things, Mary kept a collection of all of the books by and about Hemingway. I thought she would be the most likely source of Frank Maguire's biography.

"There are lots of them. Which one?"

"*Hemingway in Hollywood*."

"Frank Maguire."

"That's the one. Have you got it?"

"Of course I've got it."

She picked up a key from her desk and walked over to a glass-enclosed case where the Hemingway collection was stored. She unlocked the case, slid open one panel of the glass doors, and picked out the book, handing it to me.

"You know him?"

"Hemingway or Maguire?"

"Maguire," I said. Mary and I were not old enough to have been aware of Hemingway when he was in residence here although we'd both seen him when he made infrequent trips back from Cuba where he went to live in the forties. During his Key West years he was only a writer and not the landmark that he'd become a few years later when he'd left Key West for Cuba, but I knew that writers writing about him often used the source material here, as well as Mary, for their research.

"No," Mary said. "This book's devoted to the movies. Nothing about Key West except for that awful movie of *To Have and*

Have Not."

I opened to the author's photo on the inside of the back dust-jacket flap. The picture showed a dark-haired guy with a swarthy, round face, narrow eyes, and a nose that looked as if it had been broken. There was nothing suggesting the kind of Hollywood handsomeness that I thought Asia would have been drawn to. The picture was at least ten years old, from the publication date of the book, and though Frank Maguire wasn't pretty, his looks had a certain ruggedness even though he could only have been in his mid-twenties.

"I'd like to read this," I said, holding up the book.

Mary reached for the book as though I were going to steal it. "Then you'll have to sit your can in that chair and do it. These books don't go out of here."

"Where could I get a copy?"

"You could try the bookstore. That's where most people buy books. This one's probably out of print, but you might find a copy at the Hemingway House. They keep a large stock of stuff like this."

"Thanks, Mary. You've been helpful."

"Pshaw. A family like yours and you don't keep any memorabilia."

"I've got it. Right up here." I put a finger to my head and immediately withdrew it, reminded as I was of the image of a gun to the head.

6.

At noon a dozen people stood outside the brick wall that surrounded the grounds of the Hemingway House. A Japanese tourist was in the middle of Whitehead Street, holding up traffic while he snapped a photo. A tour bus, monstrously out of proportion to the narrow streets and neighborhood, was parked in the lot on the opposite corner of Olivia Street, its motor running, diesel fumes spilling into the humid air.

I wound my way past the crowd and walked through the open entrance gate to be greeted by Hemingway himself. Or so it seemed. A barrel-chested guy with gray hair combed forward over a broad forehead and a neatly trimmed gray beard covering his fat-cheeked face was waiting to collect money from the next swarm to tour the house while an outgoing group roamed the exterior grounds.

"I'd like to see the director," I said to Hemingway.

He looked at me as though I were about to walk off with his gate receipts. "You have an appointment?" he asked in a high-pitched voice that betrayed his appearance.

"No, I don't."

He sighed while taking twelve dollars from an elderly couple. As they walked away, speaking what sounded like German, Hemingway turned toward the house and called, "Liz!"

Seconds later a woman in a print dress came out on the porch and said, "Yes, Wallace."

"Guy wants to see Ruth." Wallace jerked a fat thumb in my direction.

"Well, send him in," Liz said.

"You can go in now," Wallace said.

"Thanks a bunch." I walked along the sidewalk toward the two-story house that was painted lime green, dodging several cats that slept on or around the sidewalk. The fabled six-toed cats reputedly descended directly from the Hemingway cats, a myth most of us who'd spent our lives here did not believe.

I stepped up on the porch and shook Liz's outstretched hand. "Don't mind Wallace," she said. "He can be a little over-bearing at times."

"But with his looks I guess he gives the place a touch of the authentic."

Liz smiled knowingly. I gave her my name and followed her inside. A central hallway ran from the front to the back of the house with the stairway up to the second floor. On the left was the dining room with a heavy wooden table surrounded by leather-covered chairs. On the right was the living room with a table lined with Hemingway books and mementos for sale.

Liz was probably in her twenties, somewhat overweight, with a maternal, almost angelic face and short hair that curled neatly against the nape of her neck. Like Wallace, she was fa-miliar; a face I'd seen many times around town but until now without any particular association. I followed her along the corridor in search of Ruth.

As I recalled, in 1961 several months after Hemingway's death, the house sold for eighty thousand dollars, ten times what his in-laws had paid for the place when they purchased it in 1931 as a wedding present. Hemingway lived in the house for almost ten years until he left for Cuba in the late thirties, paying only occasional visits to Key West thereafter. After his death the home was turned into a museum by its new owners until they sold it a year ago for more than a million dollars.

Since it was the foremost tourist attraction on the island tourists lined the streets to get in at six dollars a pop—I had to assume it was profitable.

As we passed out the back door and across the brick patio, I noticed a boxing ring, which had been erected in the side yard, and remembered my conversation with Sweetwater this morning.

Ruth was in her office out back in the former caretaker's cottage next to the studio where Hemingway had written. The office was littered with papers, magazines, and books while the smell of stale cigarette smoke hung in the small room whose one window was plugged with a wheezing air conditioner.

"This is Gideon Lowry." Liz introduced me to Ruth Clampitt, who directed the management of the house. She stood behind her littered desk, a tousled mass of thick, dark hair around a face that was heavily made up, her features exaggerated by the sequined, tinted glasses she wore over narrow eyes. She wore a man's suit jacket with padded shoulders over a shirt-blouse, and linen slacks. She took quick, nervous puffs from a cigarette, which she held in her right hand, very close to her mouth.

"Don't forget you have a lunch appointment at twelve-thirty with the board of the tourist council," Liz said before leaving.

Ruth nodded, ash from her cigarette falling across the papers on her desk. "You're not from the county health services, are you?" she asked me.

"No, I'm not."

"Well, thank God. We're bugged all of the time by one agency or another. Your name seemed familiar."

"I run an investigative service. My office is on Duval Street."

"Oh, is there a problem?" She had that air of anticipating disaster.

"I'm looking for someone, a writer who once did a biography of Hemingway."

Ruth seemed visibly relieved. "We're really a tourist attraction. I don't know if scholars would get much from us."

"I thought you might have a copy of the guy's book."

"Who is it?"

"Frank Maguire. He wrote a book called *Hemingway in Hollywood*."

"Did you look in the area where we sell books?"

"Not yet."

"It's in the front, in the main room as you come in."

"I'll check it out. Do you own the house?"

"Yes, I do. I just bought it last year."

I didn't have to ask where she was from. The New York accent had the knife-hard edges of a cold wind trapped along the avenues of Manhattan.

"How's it going?"

"Most of the time it's a major headache." Ruth paused for a moment, then added, "Without Liz I don't know how we'd manage."

"She seems very competent."

"Organized. Something, as you can see, that I am not." Ruth spread her hands above the paper-strewn desk.

"Did she come with the house?"

Ruth shook her head. "Liz came aboard when I bought the place. Wallace has been here for years."

"Wallace is a nice touch."

"Yes, he's a character."

"Is he for real?"

"You mean the looks?"

I nodded.

"We have to humor him a bit, but he takes this place seriously." She smiled. "And his looks don't hurt business any."

"I'm sure."

The phone rang. Ruth reached for it without picking up the receiver.

"There are a lot of writers around here," she said. "You should talk to them about Maguire."

"I plan to."

"Good luck."

"Don't let those six-toed cats stop breeding."

"Not a chance." Ruth smiled and lit another cigarette as she picked up the phone.

I walked back out, wending my way through cats and people, and into the house again. In the living room, up against the front windows, was a table with a collection of Hemingway books for sale. On the walls were a few dusty trophy heads and an animal-skin rug. Bookcases with Hemingway's private library, or what was reputed to be his library, were along the walls.

A black woman came over to the table and asked if she could help me.

"I'm looking for a book by Frank Maguire called *Hemingway in Hollywood*."

"Oh, yes. We got a copy of that. No one hardly ever asks for it though." She rummaged beneath the table and brought the book out.

"I'll take it. I should know you, I think."

"Marjorie Blankenship. I thought I recognized you, too. Bud Lowry?"

I nodded. "Your mother used to make the best conch fritters on the island."

Marge grinned. "She sure did. What I wouldn't give to have a batch of them right now."

"Sweetwater tells me he's going to work here, refereeing the boxing matches."

"Lordy, lordy. That man eighty years old if he is a day. What is the world coming to?"

I shook my head and paid for the book. The world of course was coming to an end sooner or later. It just didn't seem to be able to bow out gracefully.

7.

Captain Billy had once loaned money to Ernest Hemingway. It was a story my father never tired of telling. Like Patton, Hemingway was a man the captain admired, although I doubt he ever read one of his books. Unlike Phyllis, my mother, Captain Billy had little patience with reading books. What he admired in Hemingway was, of course, what my father prized in his own life: the lifelong pursuit of game fish and the solitude of being on the water. I cannot speak for Hemingway, but for Captain Billy I believe an element of the conqueror was involved in these masculine pursuits; and perhaps even the conquest of fear. Though I'd never thought of it before, it's ironic that they both ended their lives in the same way—Captain Billy's death coming just a few years prior to Hemingway's.

Phyllis knew and liked Hemingway's second wife, Pauline, whose family had provided the money to purchase the house in Key West. My mother probably sympathized with Pauline, particularly when the Hemingways separated, and Ernest left for Cuba, although more than likely Phyllis saw the parallels in their lives, too, living with two men of similar types, and from her own perspective would have probably viewed that departure as a relief.

Prior to Hemingway's time in Key West, nothing about this island held any fascination for literary types. In a sense, Hemingway put us on the map. Following his notoriety, and in his footsteps, Key West became over the years a gathering place for a variety of writers. Tennessee Williams, the antithesis of Hemingway, followed a decade or so after Hemingway's departure, and some years later an entire colony of literati called Key West home, at least during the winter months.

Back in my office I looked through the Maguire book, reading sections of it at random. I didn't have any trouble reading it. Maguire had a way of holding your attention. The characters, many of them with names I recognized from the old Hollywood, had personalities. I had no way of knowing if they were their true personalities or the product of Maguire's imagination. His wife, Asia, had said that the book was both fact and fiction. Nevertheless, I read bits and pieces of it with interest but without forming any ideas about the writer, Maguire.

I made myself a sandwich and ate it sitting at the desk, reading. I knew one writer in Key West, a man I'd done some work for at one time, and when I finished my sandwich and a cup of coffee, I called him.

Maggie Farr answered on the third ring. When I identified myself and asked for Nick, she said, "Oh, Gideon, you must be the last to know."

I frequently am. "The last to know what?"

"Nick and I separated a few months ago."

"I'm sorry to hear that." It had been several months since I'd last spoken to Nick. We were not close friends, twenty years separated us in age, but I had liked him and had seen him and Maggie frequently enough when I'd worked for him. There was a child, too, I remembered. "Is Nick still in town?"

"Yes, he lives around the corner from here, on Fleming Street. He has an unlisted number. I'll give it to you."

I wrote the number down. "All right to call now?"

"I'm sure he'll be glad to hear from you."

When I called and told him I would like to see him in connection with a case I was working on that involved another writer, Nick invited me to come by in an hour when he could take a break from his work.

I hung up and leaned back in my chair, trying to remember, in all the anecdotes Captain Billy told, if he'd ever mentioned Hemingway repaying the money he'd borrowed from my father. If he had, it would have been a story the captain would have repeated—but I don't remember ever hearing it.

8.

Nick Farr lived alone in a two-room apartment above a bike-repair shop on Fleming Street. The place was crammed with books stacked from floor to ceiling with a niche carved out in one corner where there was a desk with a computer terminal. The smell of oil and rubber from the bike shop below seemed to seep through the cracks in the scarred wooden floors and uninsulated walls. Dishes were stacked in the sink in the small kitchen adjoining the living area. A door led to the second room with its unmade bed, nothing more than a mattress on the floor, surrounded by more books. If not for the airy balcony overlooking a garden of palm trees in the back, it would have been claustrophobic.

The last time I'd seen Nick he was living in considerably better circumstances with his wife and son in a restored Conch house a few blocks from here. He had hired me to find the person who was making his life miserable by writing letters to his wife, calling on the phone at all hours of the day and night with messages about Nick's betrayal. It had gone on for several months, apparently taking its toll on his marriage, before Nick called me. He had no idea who was behind the calls, only that it was a man, and that the stories were lies. He was reluctant to go to the police for fear of attracting unwanted publicity.

I worked on the case for ten days without much success. The calls were always made from pay phones and lasted for only a few seconds. The letters were mailed from various locations outside the Keys. They were always hand-printed. I spent a lot of time with Nick talking about the various people from

29

his past who might want to cause him embarrassment, if not harm. He put together a list of names of a few people, both men and women, who might have had an ax to grind: some old acquaintances, a few of the women he'd had brief encounters with. I was looking for an unstable personality, someone who'd perhaps been through a series of bad relationships and had decided to take it out on Nick. I managed to contact a couple of people on the list, none of whom seemed likely candidates for such action.

Other than for a writing seminar Nick had taught in Miami six weeks before the notes began arriving, he had been living a solitary life, working against deadlines, with little time away from his room.

I had checked the names of the people in the seminar, talked to all of them except two who apparently no longer lived in the Miami area. The others displayed no signs of having the character traits that would lead to such tactics. Then after a couple of weeks, the letters and calls stopped. I checked with Nick, or Maggie, every three or four days for the next two weeks, until they were finally persuaded it was some fluke. They called off the investigation and I hadn't heard from them again until I called Maggie.

On the phone Nick had assured me, when telling me of his new situation, that the divorce was not the result of that incident. He seemed diminished, however, grayer than the last time we'd met, and much more on edge. After my earlier conversation with Maggie, and talking to Nick now, I had the impression that neither of them was comfortable with their decision to separate.

"Well, Gideon," Nick said, cradling a long-neck, green beer bottle to his chest as we sat on lawn chairs looking over the balcony into the dense jungle of palms, "for damn sure life doesn't march in a straight line."

Sunlight sprinkled through the rustling yellow-green leaves of palm fronds and spilled across the deck, casting long shadows from the balcony railings. "Might even take some long steps backwards now and then."

"How's the work going?" I asked.

Nick chuckled. "I'm halfway through two books, one a novel and the other a work of nonfiction that was due six months ago. I haven't got any goddamned idea how it's going." A deep furrow creased his brow. His eyes were hollow, with brooding, dark circles beneath them. He hadn't shaved in a couple of days and was as seedy as the apartment he lived in. Nick had a narrow face with short, dark hair that was thinning and flecked with gray since the last time I'd seen him. And I remembered him being heavier than he was now.

"But there's always a light at the end of the tunnel," I said.

"Oh, yes; oh, my, yes. The light. Sometimes I think Vietnam was fought just to produce that image of the light at the end of the tunnel." Nick was a veteran of that war, and I'd fought in Korea. Though we were both ex-Marines there was no camaraderie based on esprit de corps. In fact we never saw one another, but in our own distant way I suppose we both acknowledged that fraternal bond.

Nick shook his head. "You don't want to hear about alimony and child support. Taxes you know about."

"It's tough."

Nick tilted the bottle to his mouth, then raised it. "To the writer's life."

"You ever hear of Frank Maguire?"

"Of course."

"Do you know him?"

"We've met. I've talked to him a few times. I wouldn't say that I know him."

"I'm trying to find him."

"Who's he running from?"

"I don't know that he is running."

"Well, shit, Gideon. Somebody's got to be after him if you're on the case."

31

"His wife."

Nick nodded, staring into the patch of blue sky above the treetops. "Poor sod."

"Not necessarily. This wife wants to give him some money."

Nick made a sound that held only a vague resemblance to laughter. "With what kind of strings attached?"

"A divorce."

"You don't say. Just when I was beginning to believe the milk of human kindness had turned sour. Who is she? Maybe I should know her."

"Asia."

Nick turned slightly in his chair, looking over his shoulder at me in comic disbelief. "You don't mean who I think you mean, do you?"

"The singer."

"I would never have connected the two of them in a million years."

"They've been living separate lives for more than a year."

Nick shrugged and went back to his beer.

"What can you tell me about Maguire?"

"Not much. He's California, a pretty good journalist. Did a Hemingway book. It was okay. Is that the reason you got called?"

"Asia thinks he might be here."

"Why?"

"His fascination with Papa, I think. Making his pilgrimage."

"Well, he's spent time here before. The only time I met him was in Key West."

"When was that?"

"Oh, a few months ago maybe."

"But you haven't heard that he's here now."

Nick shook his head.

"Would you ask around the literary community? Casually, without advertising what's behind it?"

"I can do that. *Semper fi,* and all that crap."

I sat back, listening to Nick talk about his profession, clearly dispirited. On his way back from the kitchen with his second beer, he brought me an envelope and handed it to me. "Guess who?"

I opened the envelope and took out a single sheet of white paper, which had been folded in thirds. Inside, printed in the center of the page, was the brief message: *I'm back. Stay tuned.* I looked up at Nick. "Could it be?"

"The printing's similar. Who knows?"

"Has Maggie gotten anything?"

Nick shook his head.

"Does it mean anything to you?"

"Like a jealous husband, something like that?"

"Anything."

"No, I haven't had time to get into trouble."

"So you think it's the same person? What do you want to do about it?"

Nick shrugged and swallowed some beer. "Nothing. See where it goes. Maybe it will blow over like the last time."

We sat staring out through the wavering palms, talking desultorily, and when Nick got up to get his third beer, I made my excuses and left.

9.

"We going to get a repeat of last night?" Ronnie asked when I came into the Pier House piano bar that evening.

"Asia?" I smiled. "What do you know about her?"

"Only what I read. They're calling her another Madonna. She's a big star on MTV."

"Any men in her life?"

"She's been linked with a couple of guys in Hollywood."

"Writers?"

"What?"

"The guys in Hollywood, were they writers?"

Ronnie shook her head. "I don't think so, but I don't really know."

"You ever hear of Frank Maguire?"

Ronnie shook her beautiful mane of red hair. "I think she likes older guys. Guys your age." She winked.

"She came to see me today."

"Cool."

"I guess she'd draw quite a crowd." I looked around. Apart from some couples who sat in the lounge chairs behind us, no one was at the bar.

"I'll say. Can you pull it off?"

"I'll work on it. Right now I better go to work and see if I can drag some lost souls in here myself."

She smiled. "Do you want anything?"

"Not right now." I started for the piano.

I sat down and ran through some chords. My fingers felt stiff. I was still rusty, my rhythm uneven. You do something to me. The couples continued to chat as I played, the ice in their drinks clinking. I had no power to hypnotize anyone, no spell to break. And no voodoo to do. Asia. There was something so appealing in her voice. A kind of breathless quality that could have been the product of too much booze and too many cigarettes. Whatever it was, it had its effect. She simply mystified me.

I segued into "Night and Day," trying to recapture the moment from last night. Instead, I got lost in my reverie. Day and night. Shadow and light. Opposites. Nothing was ever quite what it seemed. I thought of photographic negative images, then saw my brother's face superimposed over my father's and felt the old torment inside me.

I played on, more Cole Porter, losing myself at the piano, and when I looked up, the few people who had been here had gone. I ended the set and walked over to the bar. "So much for dragging them in," I said to Ronnie. "Maybe I need to update my music." I said it without meaning it; I was old enough now not to have to pander to the fickle taste of the crowds.

"It's early still." She was washing glasses, plunging them on a brush fixed upside down in one of several stainless steel sinks behind the bar.

I got a club soda and wandered onto the deck overlooking the harbor. Below me, a few large tarpon flashed their silvery underbellies as they played around the pilings lit by the underwater lights. The years that these creatures had been coming here. What was it that drew them to this spot? I wondered. Something in the water? Food? Or was it just habit? The habits of a lifetime passed from one generation to another. The same kind of habits that had bound my people so tightly, kept our identity alive. Not knowledge, but habit.

A schooner loaded with tourists sailed by on its way to the dock after a sunset cruise. To the west the sky held puffy gray clouds with ragged edges, like big silhouettes, tinged with the last of the dying light. I could hear a dog barking, spiking the noise of the traffic coming from Duval Street as night settled, giving the town a different rhythm with the promise of some respite from the heat.

Something threatening was in the air. I felt it. Felt it only the way anyone who's ever given up drinking knows. It was basic fear. The fear of some uncontrollable force taking over one's life, so that nothing will ever be the same again. A certain dryness in the mouth. The palms damp, the scalp tingling.

I went back to the only refuge I knew, the piano.

10.

The next couple of days I spent in the library poring over the *Readers' Guide to Periodical Literature.* Going back month by month I found a compendium of articles by Frank Maguire in various journals spanning the last three or four years. Most of them were confined to newspapers in California, with the exception of a few pieces for the *Village Voice* and *Rolling Stone* and one article in *Esquire*—an excerpt from *Hemingway in Hollywood.* As his wife had suggested, Frank Maguire was hardly a household name.

Some of the articles were available on microfiche and I called a few of them up on the screen. They were mostly profiles of disappearing landmarks in California, along with some investigative pieces into environmental matters concerning that state. Without exception they were clearly written, if not always interesting reading the way the Hemingway book was. Still, I found myself getting caught up in the stories, even smiling occasionally when it became evident we shared a common vein of humor. With the image of his face fresh in my mind from the dust-jacket photo, I even began to feel as if I knew the guy, beginning even to like him.

Where was he?

I spent the better part of another day trying to talk to Maguire's editors and colleagues at the journals where he'd worked. I left my name and number with various people, but by the end of the day all I'd accumulated was a monstrous phone bill, and an ear red and sore from pressing a receiver to it while listening to different types of recorded banality after

37

being repeatedly put on hold. No one seemed to know a damned thing about the whereabouts of Frank Maguire.

He'd disappeared.

Asia had mentioned that he had told her he was on the brink of a big story the last time they'd talked. But even if he'd gone underground for a story, he should have surfaced by now. Unless he wasn't going to surface—ever. If I was going to find him, the key, I thought, was in that story.

I tried to reach Asia at the Casa Marina Hotel where she had told me she was staying. She wasn't in. I left a message, then fed Tom and examined the refrigerator for my own meal. There was a package of hamburger from which I could make a *picadillo*. I put an Oscar Peterson tape in the cassette radio on top of the refrigerator and began to chop up some garlic, onion, and a little green pepper-sautéing it briefly in olive oil before adding the hamburger. I put some rice on to cook and was opening a can of black beans when the phone rang.

I went into the office, sat down behind the desk, and answered it. A man's voice said, "You called about Frank Maguire today?"

"I called a lot of people about Frank Maguire today. Who's this?"

There was a hesitation at the other end of the line. "I'd rather not say," the man finally said. He sounded almost apologetic. "I know Frank, though."

"Are you with a paper?"

Another hesitation. "Yes, I am."

"But you'd rather not say which one."

"Maybe if I knew why you were looking for Frank."

"I've been hired by his wife to find him."

"The Golden Voice? I thought he and Asia had split a long time ago."

"They never finalized it."

"She getting married again?"

"I'd rather not say."

"Touché... Look, I'm with *Rolling Stone*. I didn't know Frank well, but I talked with him several times on the phone and he came to the offices once in a while when he was out here. We had lunch a couple of times. I liked him."

"He did a couple of stories for *Rolling Stone*."

"That's right."

"Was he working on another one?"

"I think so."

"Can you tell me about it?"

"It was hush-hush, which means it was big, which means we probably had an exclusive."

"Which is why nobody will talk to me."

"Probably."

"Except you."

"I'm taking a chance because I'm worried about Frank."

"When was the last time you talked to him?"

"Two months ago at least."

"Did he tell you about the story?"

"No, but I think he was using me for background research on certain parts of it."

"Can you tell me what that was?"

The hesitation again. "I'm not sure that I can. I'd like to but—"

"All right. You want to know that you can trust me first, is that it? That I'm really looking for Frank and not out to rob the story for another source."

"Well, it could be worse than that. There are probably people who wouldn't want to see this story come out. That's what I'm worried about."

"You ever heard of Nick Farr?"

"Of course."

"If he vouches for me, will you talk to me?"

"Perhaps."

"How can he reach you?"

"He can't. I'll call him."

39

I hung up and went back to the kitchen. After less than a week I had an anonymous lead to Frank Maguire. It didn't seem like much, but in this business it was more often the quality of the information that made the difference, not the quantity. It had taken half a day to find a purloined parrot a few weeks ago. From a single tip. I had no reason to believe I would get so lucky with Maguire.

The *picadillo* was overcooked and dry, with a taste of burnt garlic. Only Oscar Peterson made it palatable.

11.

After dinner I walked down to the end of the concrete pier at the foot of Duval Street. A cool, dry breeze came off the sea as I stood watching the lights on the buoys in the distance wink on and off along the main ship channel. Several feet behind me the smell of marijuana drifted up from where a young couple sat on the pier, their voices floating softly out over the water.

I stood there for a long time watching and listening to the dark, hypnotic rhythm of the water, letting my mind wander. It wandered a hundred and fifty miles up the Keys to the mainland and wondered what Casey was doing right now in Miami. She had gone there to escape the limited opportunities available in Key West where she'd been working as a graphic artist. One of life's displaced people, she'd found Key West fifteen years ago, gotten sober here, helped me get sober—and I missed her. With three marriages down the drain I didn't have any desire to go through that again, and the relaxed, commitment-free relationship with Casey had been perfect. I had not seen her since she left. I thought about calling her and went back and forth on whether there was any point in that while listening to the kids behind me, and the wavelets lapping around the edges of the concrete below me.

In the distance I could see the unmoving lights on a fleet of boats a few miles offshore. In the dark it was impossible to see their shape, but I guessed they were shrimp boats, anchoring in the advance of a weather front, their booms, like wings, extended in order to give them more stability in riding out a storm. The sight of those ships out there was as much a baro -

41

meter of impending weather as any radio forecast could be.

The sea was to my people what the prairie had been to early settlers. It had provided us with sustenance and livelihoods; over time it had shaped our lives as well as taking them. We were who we were because of this body of water that surrounded us. It had molded us, left its mark on us as clearly as any wagon track across the grasslands. The difference between these two worlds, of course, was that the prairies were now mostly gone, tamed, while the view I had was essentially unchanged—the same as it had been for me as a child, for my father, Captain Billy, and as it had been for his father and so on all the way back to the Indians who had first settled here.

My mother came from another part of the country and did not take to the sea. Except for the few times she had to take the ferry to the mainland before the highway was completed, I was sure Phyllis never set foot on a boat. For her the sea held some foreboding threat, an element of danger that she sensed but couldn't articulate. As a child I remember her climbing the widow's walk atop our home on William Street to search for the *Low Blow* on days of uncertain weather when my father was on the boat.

Captain Billy, on the other hand, thrived on the water, would have spent his life there if it hadn't been for some sense of obligation to his family. As it was, the last ten years of his life my father was seldom home. Even choosing to die on his boat.

I sought out the sea for solace, a place to come when I was feeling, as I was now, troubled and lonely. Although it didn't answer any questions, there was comfort to be gained in the endless shrug of its dark shoulders. I was no closer to finding Frank Maguire, or resolving my loneliness, but neither was I heading to the nearest bar. It had taken me the better part of my life, but I had learned something, a lesson borne in on the swell of the tide and currents with the message that things happened in their own good time and that I could do little to change their outcome.

I returned home and, after shaving, called Casey, surprised when she answered after the second ring.

"Bud, I was just thinking about you. Is everything all right?"

I knew she meant was I drinking again because as a confirmed member of AA, Casey was convinced that we couldn't make it on our own, we needed group support. I hadn't subscribed to that. I told her everything was fine. I told her about Asia coming in, and the case I was working on. I rambled, bringing her up to date on some things here, leaving her in the dark on others where we hadn't shared that part of our lives. I was aware that I was reluctant to hang up, hoping to cement something or finish it altogether.

"How are you?" I finally asked.

"I'm fine." Her voice had an ebullient quality that I had not heard in a long time. She sounded as if she were smiling. "Bud, I've met someone."

"I was wondering. Is it love?"

"Oh, I don't know that. It's too soon. But we're having a wonderful time."

"I'm glad for you." And I suppose I was. I was ten years older than Casey, and there was no future for her here. What had I expected?

She said she would like to come down some weekend, perhaps with her friend, and could we have coffee?

Of course, I told her. I felt as if I were still standing out on the pier. We talked some more, I mostly listened, and by the time we hung up, we both knew that our relationship had devolved to another level, one that would steadily slip away, like a bottle tossed into the ocean.

And it had all happened in its own good time.

12.

The following day Nick Farr called at two o'clock. It had been raining all day, with occasional gusts of wind out of the northeast, but mostly it was just a summer deluge. I was standing at the window watching the torrents of water sweeping down the gutters and the colored pennants strung around the used-car lot across the street being rain-whipped. There was no thunder, no lightning, just the steady onslaught of rain.

"Something's in the pipeline," Nick said when I answered the phone.

"Maguire?"

"He's here."

"Did you get a call from someone at *Rolling Stone?*"

"As a matter of fact. He asked about you."

"I think Maguire was doing a story for them, but they haven't heard from him in a long time either. A staffer there got nervous when I was calling yesterday."

"I sang your praises. A guy with integrity, who knows what he's doing, I told him."

"Have you talked to Maguire?"

"No. But I think I can get you an introduction."

"When?"

"Tonight soon enough?"

"Fine. I appreciate your going to all this trouble, Nick."

"I didn't break a sweat. There's a cocktail party. You can come as my guest. You'll be the only civilian."

"Civilian?"

"Strictly literary." Nick sounded vaguely British in his pro-

44

nunciation.

Nick gave me the address and I told him I would meet him there at seven. When I asked if he'd received any more anonymous notes, he said no. We hung up. I decided to get caught up on some overdue bookwork. At four o'clock it stopped raining, and the sun came out. I walked next door to the Cuban *groceria* and got a *café con leche,* chatted with the storekeeper for a while before going back to my office. Sitting at the desk, drinking the coffee from the Styrofoam cup, I thought about going down to the hardware store before they closed and getting some supplies, some paint, and painting the front of the building and eventually having the peeling letters on the windows repainted. At four-thirty the guy from *Rolling Stone* called.

"I talked to Nick Farr."

"So I heard. Did I pass the test?"

"I'm sorry. I had to take precautions." He sounded young but genuinely concerned.

"What can you tell me about Frank Maguire now?"

"I can't tell you much. I don't know the full extent of the story Frank was pursuing, but I was providing him research on an oil outfit called Globe Oil."

Globe Oil. I'd come across the name in one or two of the pieces of Maguire's I'd read on microfiche the other day. "They were doing some exploratory drilling off the coast of California," I said. "Maguire took a poke at them in print out there."

"That's right, and they didn't like it. They were small potatoes by comparison with the big names in the oil business, but they were branching out."

"Out where?"

"Florida. A few years ago they bought up some leases down there."

I thought of the protest rally that was being held in a few days. "And you think Maguire was on a crusade against Globe?"

"Oh, I think those leases were probably just the tip of the iceberg. I suspect Frank was on a much bigger story."

"Want to venture a guess?"

"Sorry. I don't have any details."

"You got any names of anyone at Globe I could talk to?" The hesitation that had been there the other day crept back over the line. "I don't want any of this coming back to me."

"I don't even know your name."

"Or *Rolling Stone*."

"I don't listen to that kind of music."

There was a sprinkle of laughter. "You'll do. The guy you'd be most interested in down there is a troubleshooter for Globe. His name's Mickey Freeman. Frank had zeroed in on him."

"Thanks. And by the way, I'm meeting with Frank tonight."

"Frank? He's there?"

"So I'm told."

There was a pause. Then, "Why didn't you say so?"

"I just did."

Another pause. "Well, how do you like that? I guess everything's cool then. Tell him to call me."

"I don't know your name."

"It's Dan Riggs."

"I'll give him the message."

It was ten to five when I drove into the parking lot of the hardware store. After the rain, vapor seemed to rise up from the pavement in thin clouds. George Lewis, the chief of detectives with the Key West police, was coming out of the store as I was going in.

"Bud, you rascal. How goes it?"

"So-so, George. How about yourself?"

"Thinking of calling it quits next year."

Lewis was a few years older than I, but we'd worked together as young patrolmen with the KWPD when I was in my twenties. "Retirement?"

"I'm a grandfather," he said, grinning. "Time to slow down,

46

enjoy myself. I don't want to be carried out of there."

George's face colored and he looked down at his shoes, re-membering, I suppose, that he'd been at the scene of my brother's death and had watched me carry Carl's body from his office.

"Good for you," I said without much enthusiasm.

"Yeah," George said, and seemed anxious to move on. "Well, good to see you, Bud. Take care of yourself."

I went inside, roamed around the air-conditioned store gathering up supplies, and drove back home feeling the weight of the years, the circle closing.

13.

A few minutes after six the front doorbell rang. I was in the kitchen trying to decide what to eat before going to meet Nick at the cocktail party when I remembered that I didn't drink so it was unnecessary to take that precaution; old habits die hard. Maybe Nick and I could have dinner afterward, I thought. Then I remembered that Nick did drink and could well not be ready to leave when I was.

I walked into the office barefoot, wearing my undershirt and khaki pants. A woman was at the door. At first I didn't recognize her; she was standing at an angle with her face turned toward the street. When I opened the door and she turned to face me, I saw that it was Asia. But not the Asia who'd been here a few days ago. This one wore a pair of baggy shorts with a wild print on them that looked like old-fashioned men's boxer shorts, a pair of espadrilles on her feet, and a T-shirt, a little whiter, but not unlike the one I had on. Her hair was loose, with a sort of teased look, the silver patch still there, but gone was the severe, starched look and the makeup. Her skin was nicely tanned, and she looked almost relaxed.

"I've tried to call a few times, but your phone's been busy," Asia said. "I decided to walk over. After all that rain it feels good to get out of the hotel."

I stepped aside to let her enter. She stood in the center of the room, shoving her hands down in the pockets of her baggy shorts, her feet nicely apart. She looked good. I told her so. Some animal magnetism seemed to surround her. It was hard to know if she was even conscious of the effect she had, or if it was just a natural byproduct of her body, like a scent that drew one closer. Whatever it was, I felt its pull.

"What is it about this place?" she asked. "You just sort of sink into the sand down here."

"And forget your troubles?"

Asia smiled. "Well, they certainly get put in perspective."

"How long are you here?"

"I'm leaving for New York the day after tomorrow. I've got a recording session then. Why? Have you found out something about Frank?"

"I'm meeting him tonight."

"That's wonderful, Gideon. What an investment you turned out to be. A real human angel. Where is he?"

"I'm going to a cocktail party for some writers where he's supposed to be. That's all I know. You've got some money coming back."

"Keep it. You've earned it."

A thousand dollars for about five days' work. All jobs should be so easy to come by. "What do I tell Frank?"

"I want him to sign some papers and then I'll give him a check."

"Shall I ask him to call you?"

"I'd rather you handled it all." Asia withdrew a hand from her pocket and touched my arm. "You're sweet, Gideon. Is there a Mrs. Lowry?"

"Three of them, and as far as I know all of them have dropped the Lowry and none of them ever thought of me as sweet. Or a human angel."

Asia laughed. It was a pleasant sound. And she hadn't had a cigarette since she came in.

"Are you trying to keep a low profile while you're here?"

She smiled. "That wouldn't be easy. Besides, the paper is doing a story in tomorrow's edition."

"Well, if you're not doing anything, I'm back at the Pier House tomorrow night if you'd like to stop in."

49

"And sing?"

"I'd like that."

"Mr. Sandman," she sang enticingly, "bring me a dream."

I smiled. "Sure, and maybe something by Cole Porter."

"I'll try. No promises, but I will try to stop by. You deserve that much."

I waved a hand through the air as if to ward off the thought. The product of deserving hadn't always been a reward. "Trying is acceptable."

When she had gone, I went into the bathroom to shave, whistling: Make her the sweetest thing I have seen.

Once again I felt that certain unease, a kind of tension that I'd associated with calamity so often that it was like the arthritic's portent of rain. I could sense it on the horizon, but of course I was powerless to stop it. Just as I'd been powerless to prevent the deaths of my father and brother. I was a living bellwether, a harbinger of bad tidings. I bore the burden like a bell around the neck of a leper. So my darkling thoughts proceeded as I prepared to go out on quest into the night.

14.

A white picket fence ran along the edge of the sidewalk and back down the sides of a lawn not much larger than an oversize postcard to a white, gabled house with dark green, louvered shutters thrown open against the white siding of the house. Yellow light fell from the windows onto the porch and across the lawn. Laughter spilled like rain from the open front door of the house. I stood on the sidewalk outside, waiting for Nick Farr. A few people glanced at me curiously as they opened the gate in the picket fence and went in.

Nick showed up at seven-twenty without apology. He had on worn jeans, scuffed deck shoes, and a wrinkled khaki shirt, a section of the shirttail peeking from the back waistband of his jeans.

"I didn't mention to anyone who you are or why you're here," Nick said as we walked through the gate and up to the porch. "If I don't see Maguire, I'll introduce you to someone who knows him and then you're on your own."

"Thanks. Dinner's on me afterwards if you want."

He nodded. "I'll probably be ready to bail out, too, unless there's some lonely lady I can't drag myself away from."

We went in the front door and down a hallway toward the chatter and laughter at the back of the house. There was an open living room with minimal furnishings, glossy hardwood floors, and a pair of French doors that opened onto a deck and pool area. A bar had been set up in one corner of the deck, and we made our way to it, Nick pausing to shake hands here and there, a few more curious glances thrown my way, but I didn't see anyone I knew.

Forty years ago I probably knew the owners of this place, but that was long before anyone thought about sandblasting the wood walls or putting a swimming pool where chickens had once been raised.

At the bar Nick asked for a beer from the young guy in a tux shirt who was dispensing drinks. I got my ritual club soda and squeezed a wedge of lime in it. Clusters of people stood around the pool, mostly men.

"I don't see Maguire, but there's Ben Kantor." Nick pointed with his beer bottle in the direction of the far corner of the pool. "Ben's a writer, been around for years, and knows Frank."

I followed Nick around the pool where a bald guy was talking to a woman in a silk blouse with a large silvery earring dangling from the lobe of one of her ears.

"Ben," Nick said, coming up on the two of them. "I want you to meet someone."

Kantor stepped back from the woman he'd been talking to and made room for us. "This is Gideon Lowry," Nick said. "Ben Kantor. And Jocelyn Beatty."

I shook hands with Kantor and nodded at Jocelyn. Kantor was short, round, probably about my age, bald except for a dark line of hair about an inch wide that banded his head from ear to ear. He wore thick-lensed glasses and looked like an academic in a rumpled seersucker jacket and tie.

"Jos, I didn't know you were in town. You got a minute?"

Nick took his lonely lady by the elbow and propelled her toward the bar.

"You a writer, Mr. Lowry?" Ben Kantor asked. "I'm unfamiliar with your name."

"No, I'm a private investigator."

Kantor's eyes flickered momentarily with interest. "Oh. That's..." He seemed to search for a word. Finally he found it: "Refreshing. We don't see many detectives at these soirees."

"You don't live in Key West?"

"I usually come down in the winter for six months and stay in the compound here. I came back now for the Hemingway festival."

"What compound?" I asked.

Kantor smiled. His lips were papery thin, his face crossed with a delicate webbing of broken veins just below the skin surface along his cheeks. "Amazing, isn't it, what's tucked away from the streets on this island. Behind this fence"—he motioned to a stockade fence that surrounded the pool area and was itself nearly obscured by thick tropical foliage"—there's half a dozen cottages that get used primarily in the winter by us transplants. Snowbirds, I think you call us."

"That's convenient."

"Yes, if somewhat isolated."

"But if you're a writer, I suppose it's a quiet place to work."

"Yes, it offers that, plus some social life, even if it's with the same faces."

"What kind of writing do you do?"

"The boring kind. Financial and business matters. I don't really fit in with the creative element here. I've just been around so long I'm part of the woodwork." Kramer waved a small hand with manicured nails. "But enough of me. What about you? You're out in the world doing interesting things. I'd rather hear about that."

"I was hoping to meet someone."

"Really? You mean this isn't a social call?" Kantor sounded faintly excited.

"No, I'm working."

"And who are you looking for?"

"Frank Maguire."

"Oh." Kantor's eyes seemed to lose some of their luster. "Is that why Nick brought you to me?"

I said it was.

Kantor looked around. "Well, let's see. I don't think Frank has made an appearance, or even if he intends to. Mind if I ask why you want to meet him?"

"His wife hired me to find him. Do you know her?"

"I don't know much about Maguire's personal life."

"What about Globe Oil? Know anything about them?"

Kantor smiled. "Oh, well, yes. I'm familiar with Globe. Why?"

"Just curious. I heard that Frank was pursuing a story on them and I wondered if that was why he was here."

"I'll see if I can find him and you can ask him yourself," Kantor said, turning away.

I watched him negotiate his way through a disguised opening in the fence. Thirty, maybe forty people were milling around, passing from one group to another, smiling, nodding, very comfortable, as if they'd known each other for years. And maybe they had. I had the impression of being in on a party that had been going for years, without end. People shifted and sauntered around the pool, changing groups, exhausting conversation, on the hunt for something more exciting. I hung back in the shadows, surveying the crowd, searching for Nick. I caught sight of him inside the kitchen, leaning against the refrigerator, the ever-present bottle of beer dangling from his fingers. I went to tell him of my success.

15.

Nick was talking to Jocelyn, the woman who'd been with Kantor when we were introduced.

"Gideon"—Nick waved his beer bottle in my direction when I walked up—"how did you and Ben make out?"

"Fine." I smiled at Jocelyn. She was pretty, not tall, with curly ringlets of hair that came down the side of her face in front of her ears. Each time she moved her head the single earring bobbed in and out of the tangle of curls.

"Any luck with Maguire?"

"Frank Maguire?" Jocelyn asked.

"Do you know him?" Nick asked.

"Of course." She smiled brightly, an even row of white teeth.

"Gideon wants to talk to him."

"Why didn't you say so? He's been drinking. I'm not sure he was even going to come, but I'll see if I can coax him over."

"You might have better luck than Kantor," Nick said, grinning.

Jocelyn turned and walked away.

"Who is she?" I asked.

Nick shrugged. "A groupie. She's written some poetry, but basically she just seems to work the fringes of the literary set wherever she can find them."

"And she manages to make a living at it?"

"She was married to one of Hemingway's grandsons for a while. I believe she was able to cash in on that."

"Nice."

Nick downed some beer. "Jocelyn's a bit of a scammer maybe, but otherwise she's okay."

"She's here for the festival?"

"She and I are going to be judges of the look-alike contest," Nick scoffed. "And she's a reader in the short-story contest. Let's get another drink."

We walked to the bar where the bartender had worked up a sweat and refilled my cup with soda. Nick took another beer. Moments later, I saw Jocelyn walking across the pool deck toward us and talking with a stocky guy who was barefoot and had on a pair of rumpled khaki shorts and a T-shirt. Nick had seen them, too. "Frank Maguire," he said.

We moved away from the bar, making room for them.

"Here he is," Jocelyn said. "Frank, you know Nick Farr, don't you?"

"Yeah, we met once. When was it? Six months ago, I think." Frank's voice was raspy, his words coming out in staccato like bursts.

"Something like that," Nick said, shaking hands with Maguire.

I'm not sure I would have recognized Maguire from his dust-jacket photo. He had a few days' growth of beard and his curly hair was short and uncombed. He wore wire-rimmed glasses, and though he couldn't have been much more than thirty-five, there was a certain resemblance to Hemingway, I thought. Whether it was studied or natural was hard to tell.

"This is Gideon Lowry," Jocelyn said, looking at Maguire strangely, I thought, as though with mixed emotions.

We shook hands before Maguire turned his attention to the bar, ordering a rum and Coke. When he had his drink, the four of us stepped over to a corner of the deck that was unpopulated.

Maguire tilted his drink back and then held the cup grasped in his fist close to his chest. "I saw Kantor," he said to me. "Says you were asking about me."

56

"Asia's in town. She asked me to find you."

Maguire laughed, more of a rumble from deep in his chest. This was not at all the man I'd imagined while reading his early articles on microfiche in the library the other day. I had the feeling this Maguire was a poser. I had a keen sense for impostors because I had grown up with one. My father. Captain Billy had assumed a cloak of arrogance in an effort to hide his deficiencies. He became a caricature, a stereotype. Though all of us in our family probably discovered this for ourselves over the years, we never discussed it and certainly never confronted him. No one dared interfere with his choice of image.

Like Captain Billy, Frank Maguire was creating an image for himself. One that I was sure was unnatural. I wondered why.

"Don't tell me," Maguire said. "She wants a divorce."

I nodded. I wasn't sure Frank, or Asia, would want the details of this made public. "There are some stipulations that we should probably discuss."

Maguire finished his drink and looked from Jocelyn to Nick. "Well," he said, rising up on the balls of his feet, "let's go discuss them."

Following Maguire through the maze of people and domestic hazards was like being in a blood-darkened bullring, watching as he worked the crowd as if he were a picador, alone and aloof in his superior position, wearing down each bull. Maguire reached out to some, ignoring others, pausing occasionally to offer information, a personal anecdote, delivered in a clandestine way to another favored subject. He could be cruelly oblivious; caustic one minute, and pandering the next.

There was something about him, something more elusive than arrogance, a kind of instinct for cruelty. Maguire required attention, I thought, and the way he insured it was by acting like a cad. He was sweating profusely, his T-shirt darkened, his face beaded with moisture. Or perhaps he was just drunk.

I was relieved when we finally stepped through the gate in the fence and into the relative quiet of the empty compound.

16.

Half a dozen small cottages, all similarly constructed, formed a sort of semicircle around a gravel walkway bordered by palm trees with ground lighting illuminating their drooping fronds. A pool, so small that more than two people in it would have required intimacy, was in the middle of the circle, an underwater light somehow seeming to further diminish its size.

Frank stepped up on the narrow porch of a cottage at the far end of the row and stood beneath a yellow porch light while holding the screen door open with his foot and using the muted light to get a key into the lock in the door. "Trouble with this place," he said, "you got to be looking over your shoulder all the time. Nobody'd take a dime off your dresser, but leave an idea lying around and it'll be gone."

He opened the door and we went in. The place smelled slightly of mildew and sweat and booze. A light was on in the small front room, which held a few pieces of furniture, a cane couch, a desk, and a couple of chairs, with some tropical pastels on the walls. Newspapers were stacked on the floor next to the couch. Papers were piled on the desk beside a portable typewriter.

"Want a drink?" Frank asked.

"No, thanks."

Frank looked at me suspiciously and went into the next room where I heard him putting ice in a glass. He carried the drink back in and sat down heavily at the desk, straddling the chair backward.

"How long have you been here?" I asked, sitting on the

couch.

"Couple of months."

"Apparently you've been keeping a low profile."

"I came here to do research on a project. There's no reason to advertise it all over the place."

"Globe Oil?"

"What's Asia been feeding you?"

"She hired me to find you. I did some research of my own that connected you to Globe. With the recent interest in off-shore drilling here it wasn't too much of a leap to think you might be on a story. For, say, *Rolling Stone?*"

Frank smiled. "All right, you get points for good gumshoe-ing. You found me, but don't gloat."

"Dan Riggs would like you to call him. I think he wants to talk about Mickey Freeman."

"All right, go ahead and gloat! Globe Oil isn't my main interest in life any longer. Anyway, I thought we were here to talk about Asia."

"The divorce settlement."

"My, and we've been having such a fine time apart. Why does she want to ruin it?"

"She says you need money."

"God, not even sex. How common of the bitch."

"She's ready to give you a settlement."

"Big of her. What kind of a settlement?"

"Fifty thousand dollars when you sign the papers."

"That's it? No strings?"

"No strings."

"Why do I smell a rat?"

I didn't know. I didn't want to know. "What do I tell her?"

"Tell her I want to see her."

"You'll do it?"

"I want to see her first." Frank finished his drink.

I stood up. I'd done my job, earned a thousand dollars even though the burdensome bell around my neck rang in alarm; I smelled that rat, too. "I'll tell her," I said.

I walked back across the grounds and reentered the party. Nick was at the bar talking to several people, among them Ben Kantor. I didn't see Jocelyn. When he saw me, Nick came over.

"What about Maguire?"

"What about him?" I asked.

"He's phony as plastic fruit."

"He seemed to be playing Hemingway."

"Playing him! He's writing him."

"What do you mean?"

"Jocelyn told me she gave him an uncompleted Hemingway manuscript she'd managed to get her hands on."

"From her ex-husband, Hemingway's grandson?"

"She didn't say where it came from."

A few years after Hemingway's death, a trunk containing some of his possessions was unearthed in Sloppy Joe's bar. Among the stuff, I recalled, was some unfinished writing Hemingway had left there. It was published, as were a couple of other works that came to light, some years later. Still, it seemed by now that source would have been tapped out.

"Do you believe her?" I asked Nick.

"I'm not sure. She's capable of cooking something up."

"For what purpose?"

"Money, what else."

"What's Maguire's involvement?" When I'd asked about the *Rolling Stone* project, he'd said he was onto something else. This must have been it.

"Edit and finish it and then sell it for a fortune. It will make his name."

"Only if he changes it to Hemingway," I said.

"The son of a bitch will probably do that, too. We're all going over to the Hemingway House for the boxing match. You coming?"

I said not. I didn't care to see what they would do to Sweetwater, and I had had enough. Maguire was posturing, playing a role, building himself into his obsession, reinventing himself in a manner that was not pretty. Or maybe, as Nick said, he just saw a way of making a quick buck. Either way I was feeling disillusioned. With Asia for thinking she could buy off her husband. With Maguire for selling out his talent. With the entire phony lot of them. I had seen this once before with Captain Billy. I said goodnight and escaped home to my own private obsessions.

17.

"MTV'S Asia in Key West." The next morning's *Herald* devoted half of the Keys section of the paper to Asia's "retreat," as she called it. "It's so easy just to sink into the sand down here," she said. She did not mention Frank Maguire in the article. There were two photographs of Asia alone on a pier, one as she sat topless, taken from the back with her face tilted upward and turned in profile to the camera, her eyes closed, a slight smile on her lips. The other had her standing, leaning over the pier railing, dressed in a filmy wraparound beach outfit with a thong bikini underneath and her butt clearly defined.

"What that paper be printin' these days," Sweetwater said, sitting down at the counter next to me.

"How you doing, Sweets?" I finished the remains of the poached egg and grits, pushed my plate aside, and reached for my coffee. "How did the fight go last night at the Hemingway House?"

"I didn't see you there."

"I didn't make it. I promise you I'll be there for the next one."

"If there be a next one."

"Why wouldn't there be?"

"You didn't hear? A man got himself killed over there last night."

I felt a wave of apprehension pass through me, the arrival of the portent that had come the other day and was as unsettling as thunder. "There was nothing in the paper."

"Must have happened too late to make the mornin' paper."

"Who was it?"

"A writer man, I don't remember his name."

I nodded and picked up my check, the apprehension turning now to dread. "What do you know about it?"

"He got himself shot in the pool house is all I know, Bud."

I stood up. "I've got to go. Take care, Sweets."

His eyes stared at me, his face seemed pained, contorted. "You know something about this, Bud?"

"I don't know. I might." I went home and called George Lewis, the captain of detectives at the Key West Police Department. George was out of the office. I asked his secretary if the name of the murder victim at the Hemingway House last night had been released. She stepped away from the phone a minute and came back and said, "Yes, his name's Frank Maguire."

I knew him all right. And I knew his wife and a few of his friends. It had been an easy job, too easy, I thought, and I'd been paid too much money for it. Now, I sensed I was going to be forced to earn that money. I left a message for George Lewis to call me, then I tried to reach Asia at the hotel.

Asia wasn't in her room, but I'd no sooner hung up the phone than she walked in the door. She looked grim, her eyes scared, tension lines creasing the corners of her mouth.

"Have you heard?"

"Yes," I said. "Just now."

"What happened?"

"I don't know. The person I needed to talk to at the police department was out. I don't have any details."

"Did you see Frank last night?"

"Yes. We talked. I told him what you wanted. He said he wanted to see you."

"How did he seem?" Asia was clenching a handkerchief in her fist.

"Drunk. Somewhat belligerent."

"Oh, God! Frank could never drink."

I didn't say anything.

"Gideon, I don't want to be drawn into this."

"There was no mention of your connection with Frank in the paper, but you were married to him. When the police learn that, they're going to want to question you."

"Will you handle it for me?" she pleaded. "I have to go back to New York."

"Not until tomorrow, right?"

"Yes, but I don't want to get tied down, and there is nothing I can tell the police."

"Let me see what I can find out. Where will you be?"

"In the hotel. I'll wait for you to call."

I nodded. Asia came around behind the desk and put her hand on my face. "You really are a human angel, Gideon." She smelled of jasmine. "Help me through this."

A shiver ran through my body like a gust of winter wind. It was almost ninety degrees outside and I was sweating, but when Asia left, a chill lingered from her touch. The phone rang. I picked it up expecting to hear George Lewis's voice, but it was Ben Kantor, the writer I'd talked to last night at the party where I'd met Maguire.

"This is dreadful," Kantor said. "Can you do anything?"

"The police are investigating. What can I do?"

"I don't know. You met him, you knew something of what he was doing."

"Very little. He seemed reluctant to talk about it."

"The business with Globe Oil, you mean?"

"Yes."

"Let me fill you in."

Kantor talked about Globe and Mickey Freeman. Mostly Mickey Freeman, who had worked his way up Globe's corporate ladder beginning as a young wildcatter in the oil fields of Texas and Oklahoma in the 1950s. He now flew around the country in Globe's leased jet, their personal emissary, a lobbyist who dined with legislators in the state capitals as well as in Washington. He had full authority to act on behalf of Globe-

cutting deals, passing out money, and twisting arms whenever necessary. Beneath the Texas-size charm and bullshit, Kantor explained, was a legendary instinct for getting what he—and Globe—wanted, and a ruthless vindictiveness when he didn't.

Despite his age and the company he kept, Mickey Freeman still favored the Western clothes of his youth, particularly bolo ties and expensive cowboy boots. Frank Maguire had been pursuing him on and off for nearly a decade, mostly in California, and now in Florida. With the Hemingway project under way, Frank had another, greater interest, but he had been advising Kantor on the Globe story.

"Why is Freeman so important?" I asked when Kantor was done.

"Because I saw him at the Hemingway House last night."

18.

I went to the library and began researching Globe. By noon I had amassed several articles, once again using the *Readers' Guide,* and photocopying them from the microfiche. A couple of the articles were ones I'd seen earlier, written by Frank Maguire, although there wasn't nearly as much overlapping as I had expected.

As Kantor had told me, Globe had its genesis in Texas and the Oklahoma panhandle in the 1950s when they'd done some successful wildcatting. Despite the competition from the corporate giants in the oil industry, Globe survived. In the sixties they managed the lowball bid, winning the right to put an exploratory offshore well in Louisiana state waters. Following that success they had bought several offshore leases in California, and later Florida—leases they'd had to sit on after a disastrous oil spill off the coast of California made questionable the putting at risk of the coastlines of tourist-dependent states.

In that instance Globe seemed to have suffered financial setbacks. Only sporadic articles appeared from the mid-seventies to the present, their name usually mentioned only in passing in some historical context.

There was no reference in any of this to Mickey Freeman, Globe's troubleshooter in Florida.

From the library I biked home, deposited the papers, and picked up the keys to the Conchmobile—the 1973 Buick Electra that drank some oil and was pitted with rust, but still performed when I needed to get beyond bicycle range.

I drove out to the end of the Key, New Town, where the

shopping malls had spawned in the sixties on land that had once been underwater until the developers used fill to create a strata for the hideous eyesore of plazas and vast parking lots, cineplexes, and fast-food joints along with the cheap chain motels that were the first view new arrivals got of the island. Serving to remind them that we weren't so different down here after all.

I pulled in and parked in one of the more modest plazas that was listed in the phone book as the address for Key West's only brokerage firm. I left the windows down on the Buick and walked across the parking lot. An empty McDonald's bag skittered across the asphalt, carried by the light breeze coming off the Gulf. Picking up the bag, I deposited it in a nearby Dumpster.

I found the brokerage office on the second floor of an ice cream shop that was situated between an interior designer and a chiropractor. I walked up the outside stairway and along the balcony to their office.

It was a three-desk firm, each desk with its own computer terminal, the decor in tan and brown, the sweetish smell of pipe smoke hanging in the air. There was a small waiting room with pamphlets about the firm, and I was glancing through one of those when a silver-haired guy in a short-sleeved shirt with a red-and-blue-striped tie came out. He had thick salt-and-pepper eyebrows above black-framed glasses. He asked how he could help.

"I'm interested in some information on Globe Oil."

"Globe?" He frowned. "Follow me. Let's see what we can pull up on the computer."

We went back to one of the desks, past another broker who was on the phone. I sat down in a vinyl-padded stainless-steel chair beside the desk and watched as he punched a few computer keys, then picked up a pipe from an ashtray as he waited.

"Here we go," he said with the unlit pipe firmly between his teeth. "They're at twenty-seven and a quarter, down an eighth from yesterday's close."

Although I'd never bought a stock, I knew he was quoting the market shares. I didn't want to appear entirely ignorant. "I'd like some detail on the company. Their portfolio, maybe."

"Sure, no problem. Let me dig around here a minute. Get their value line. See what Standard and Poor's has on it." I was entirely ignorant. I'd heard of Standard and Poor's, but that didn't help; I'd also heard of the theory of relativity. My brother, Carl, would have been conversant in this stuff.

I told him I had a personal interest in Globe and he nodded. Moments later the computer printer spit out some sheets of paper, which he handed me. They might as well have been in Greek.

"I'm going to need some help here."

The broker looked at me, his eyebrows arching above his glasses. He lit his pipe and said, "No problem." Ten minutes later I'd had a short course in stock jargon without learning anything that helped shed light on Globe's mystery.

"That make sense?" the broker asked.

"It makes sense. But it doesn't tell me anything I want to know."

"What do you want to know?"

"About Globe Oil. What kind of a company they are. More than just their financial status."

The broker chuckled, a thin stream of smoke curling above his head. "A little insider information. Is that it?"

"If you've got any."

"Let me think. It seems I have heard rumors that they've diversified over the years."

"Diversified?"

"Bought into other companies. Maybe even a couple of leveraged buyouts."

"Tell me how that works."

"Well, one company buying another, usually on margin, without putting up any money, simply with the assets of the buying company as a kind of promissory note. Fairly common stuff back in the eighties."

"What's the advantage?"

"No immediate capital outlay. If the purchased company can be turned around, showing a quick profit, then it's a smart move. A lot of those leveraged buyouts, however, resulted in both companies going under."

"That doesn't seem to be the case with Globe."

"No, but you saw their five-year financial report. It's only been in the last two years that things have been on the upswing for them. They nearly doubled their volume of trading the last year."

"What was the diversification? What did they get into?"

"I believe it was largely in the entertainment industry. Both in California and Florida."

"Anything specific come to mind?"

"I would have to do some checking." He paused to relight his pipe. "You want to invest?"

"Maybe. I don't know if it would be with Globe, but I recently came into some money. I would consider investing."

"Give me a few days." He reached for a business card in a tray on his desk and handed it to me. I stood up and put it in my pocket. We shook hands as the phone rang.

I left the office and walked across the parking lot to the Buick, feeling even more at a loss than when I'd arrived.

19.

During my brief two-year tenure as a Key West cop when I'd returned from Korea in 1956, George Lewis and I had worked together as patrolmen. Although we had never been close, we had known each other so long now that we were like relatives who sometimes labored in each other's company; suffice it to say we had our differences.

When George returned my call in mid-afternoon, he sounded harassed. "What's your interest in the Maguire death?" he demanded.

"I was doing some work for a client who was involved with him."

"Does that client have a name?"

"Not at the moment."

"Look, Bud, this is a murder investigation. I'm not going to sit around playing cat and mouse with you."

"Tell me what you've got. I'll pass the word along."

"What we've got is a dead man. Shot in the head with a twelve-gauge from close range."

"What time?"

"Between midnight and two this morning, the coroner thinks."

"When was Maguire found?"

"Seven-thirty this morning. Groundspeople found him in the pool house."

"Any leads?"

"Yeah, a couple hundred of them as a matter of fact. That was the estimated crowd at the party last night."

"Good luck."

"And a little help from our friends. Look, we've closed the house down for the time being. You any idea what that means in gate receipts? Especially this week. I'm under some pressure here, Bud. If you've got information, anything, you'd be smart to volunteer it. Don't make me have to come after you."

"I'll pass the word to my client." I pictured George sitting in the cubicle of his office, his feet propped on the desk, surrounded by pictures of his grandkids. Thinking about his retirement.

"You've ruled out suicide?" I thought of Frank Maguire carrying his Hemingway imitation to the extreme.

George's tone changed. "We haven't ruled anything out, but Wes doesn't think so."

We hung up and I called the coroner's office and asked for Wes Hutton. He was out of the office. I left a message and rode over to the Casa Marina to talk to Asia.

She opened the door to her suite wearing a full-length white silk robe belted at the waist. She put her arms around me, pressing her body against mine. "My hero," she said. I followed her across the thick pile carpeting feeling somewhat shaky for a hero.

Asia sat down on a couch, reclined, tucking the robe loosely around her thighs, leaving her lower legs and feet exposed. "I'll be just a sec," she said, donning a pair of plastic goggles that had a small darkened lens in the center of each eyepiece. A sunlamp was on a stand at the end of the couch, angled over her face.

I moved over to the window where heavy drapes had been parted enough to let some light in and looked out over the green lawns dotted with palm trees down to the swimming pool and beyond to the beach, where colored canopies stretched along the sand, while behind me Asia was getting her tan from a lamp.

"I can't go out on the beach anymore," Asia said, as if she'd

71

read my mind. "I spend all my time signing autographs and being stared at."

"The cost of fame."

"I'll pay it, but on my terms. What did you find out?"

I turned from the window and looked back at her. She was still stretched out, her face ghostly under the glow of the lamp. I told her what I'd learned from George Lewis.

"I'm so nervous."

"What's there to be nervous about?"

"Having to answer a lot of questions."

I stared out the window. "I didn't tell the police about you. They're going to want to know. They'll find out sooner or later. It's going to go better for both of us if it's sooner."

Asia reached up and turned off the sunlamp but continued to lie on the sofa with the plastic goggles on, one arm thrown back over the armrest. I turned and watched her reach with the other hand and pick up a cigarette butt from the ashtray on the coffee table next to her. She took a cigarette lighter from the pocket of her gown and lit the butt. It wasn't a cigarette. The cloying smell of marijuana quickly filled the room. "Want some?" Asia held the joint over her head.

"No, thanks." I said it with more determination than I felt. Something in her pose, the languid sensuality, her blinded eyes, spurred me to join her. Instead, I stood silently and watched her smoke, holding the end of the joint pinched between her nails until there was nothing but a flyspeck left, which she dusted from her fingers back into the ashtray.

Asia stretched one leg, slowly running her hand down her white-clad thigh. The air in the room was sweet and heavy; sunlight from the window made a perfect rectangle on the pale carpeting, and the only sound was the murmur of air being blown in through the air-conditioning ducts.

It seemed like a timeless moment. I took a deep breath, aware that for some seconds I'd been holding it in.

"What?"

"I didn't say anything," I said.

"Then you were thinking something. I heard it."

"Do you read minds, too?"

Asia giggled. "Gideon, come over here."

I walked away from the window and came around to stand at the end of the couch. I shifted my weight, staring at her eyeless eyes.

"Would you hand me that nail polish. It's on the table over there." I looked where she pointed, a small vanity along one wall filled with makeup paraphernalia—nail files, bottles of polish, lipsticks, and skin creams. I walked over, found the nail polish, and brought it back to her. She took it and began shaking the bottle. Then, she removed the goggles and sat up.

I watched as she pushed a cup with the residue of a *con leche* clinging to its sides out of the way on the coffee table in front of her, fluffed the robe around her legs, and put one foot up on the table.

"Do you still want me to come and sing tonight?" She began to paint her toes.

"If you're up to it." I watched in silence, feeling a surge of blood coursing through my body. I wanted to turn and walk out but I couldn't.

"Life goes on, doesn't it?"

When she finished with one foot, she gently eased it off the table and put the other one up, her robe shifting as she did, and for a brief instant before she gathered up the folds I glimpsed that she wore nothing beneath the robe, not even a covering of hair between her legs.

"We've got to enjoy ourselves, don't we?" Asia asked.

I was dumb and my feet felt as if they were buried in soft concrete. I shook my head. "What about the police?"

"Believe me, Gideon, I have nothing to hide, but right now is not the time for me to talk to them. I can't do it."

"Fine, but I don't know if I can protect you."

"A day, that's all I ask."

I nodded. "I'll try."

Asia smiled. "I'm sorry I can't walk you to the door. I have to let the paint dry." Her face was tilted up, and something in her expression and the long, white column of her neck made her seem vulnerable. "Kiss me."

I leaned over and kissed the cool flesh of her cheek, my heart pounding. Then I let myself out and took a couple of deep breaths before I tackled the stairs down to the lobby. It seemed to take forever.

20.

There was an audience that night at the club. I played Brubeck and some Erroll Garner, but it was a request for "Moon River" that brought the applause.

I was into the second set, working over "Sophisticated Lady," when a woman walked in. Dazzling. I had followed her progress through the window as she slinked along the outside deck. She wore a plain black, full-length gown of some shimmery material that flared slightly about midway down her calves. Around her neck was a single strand of pearls. Against the light and the shadows her skin was white, almost translucent. She was white-blond, her hair curling slightly just over her shoulders, settling over the thin spaghetti straps of her dress. Everyone, it seemed, turned and stared when she went by on her way to the bar, taking a seat at the end nearest the piano. Although something was vaguely familiar, I didn't recognize her.

Ronnie came by a few minutes later with a fresh club soda and put it on the piano. She was grinning. "You did it," she whispered in my ear.

"Did what?"

"Brought in Asia."

I turned and looked at the blonde. "Her?"

"Huh-uh," Ronnie replied, turning to go back to the bar.

I finished the number and took a quick break.

"Quite a disguise," I said.

She smiled. Her expression was different from anything I'd seen in our three previous encounters. As if, behind the clothes and the wig, she really had become another person. I was affected by her in the same way I'd been affected by her before, caught off guard by the changeable personality.

"Gideon, you really are so sweet. In a provincial sort of way."

Even her voice, the way she spoke was different.

"And you play well. You've got a certain style." She laid the palm of her hand briefly across my cheek.

"Care to sing?"

"Well, I didn't dress like this to sit alone at the bar."

"What do you want to do?"

She thought for a moment. "How about 'I Get Along Without You Very Well'?"

I nodded, smiling. Indeed you do. And going back onto the stage, I picked up the hand mike inside the piano. "Ladies and gentlemen, I give you Asia."

She stepped up onto the platform stage and took the mike to applause and a long, shrill whistle. She smiled, tapping the palm of one hand against her leg, humming softly, her face turned away from the mike toward me. I struck a chord. She nodded.

I get along without you very well.

Sometimes she spoke the words more than singing them, her eyes closed, her body motionless. The audience was hushed, the room flooded with her voice, and the shared recognition of pain and loss.

I segued into "I Love You for Sentimental Reasons." People began coming in as if her voice had been a messenger on angel's wings flying out into the night, a herald of heaven. The bar filled up, then the remaining tables; finally people were standing leaning against the walls and each other. They shouted, cheered, whistled, and clapped at the end of each number. Behind the bar Ronnie was grinning her head off.

Asia sang for half an hour. She did "Mack the Knife" and "Lily Marlene" in a throaty Dietrich rendition, ending once again with "Night and Day." And when she was done, the whole place erupted. Asia dropped the mike, dangling it by the cord against her leg, leaned against the curve of the baby grand, and smiled, lowering her head. When she looked up, she glanced at me, winked, and held her hand out. I stood up. She came into my arms, pressing her body against mine while looking over her shoulder at the audience. They went wild.

"How do I get out of here?" she whispered in my ear.

"The service entrance. I'll take you." I led her by the hand, behind the bar. Ronnie said something about an autograph. People were shouting to her while Asia kept the smile pasted on her face until we stepped beyond the bar to a short hallway and a door that opened onto a concrete area of Dumpsters and the smell of rotting garbage. It was an unceremonious exit, but it avoided any hassles with people.

Asia pulled off the wig and her dark hair was damp with sweat, an angry red line where the wig had bit into her flesh at the hairline. Her face now looked drawn and vulnerable. She had changed yet again.

She stood leaning into the doorjamb, a streetlight behind her, silhouetting her figure. "Thank you, Gideon, you've been wonderful as usual."

"You're still leaving?"

She nodded.

"You're out of my hands now. I can't protect you, you know that."

Asia looked wan. "I just can't think about any of that right now."

I started to tell her once again that she was making a mistake, that she should take care of this before leaving, but looking at her standing framed in the doorway, the wig in her hands, the sickening smell surrounding us, I decided I could no longer advise her. I didn't work for her. She was a big girl, on her own now.

She smiled and touched her forefinger to her lips as she

stepped away, holding the finger toward me, and the door slowly closed.

I walked on jellied legs back to the piano and finished the night. It wasn't the same. I heard only the noise of people talking, laughing; the clink of glasses, and the whir of the cocktail blender behind the bar. The music had gone out the back door.

At two o'clock in the morning stars hung like tears in the sky. For more years than I cared to count I'd been watching this miracle, these ancient dead stars whose light was just reaching my eyes. Coming home at this hour from a club date, I could invariably count on the weight of the night, the burden of a dead star, to bring on funereal thoughts—a tragicomic nocturnal vigil that up until a couple of months ago I'd been able to ascribe to alcohol.

I always took the back streets, which allowed the ambient darkness to work its magic. In the years when I was drinking, I often saw the faces of my family pinned to those stars—Captain Billy swaggering out of the night sky, his face crusty as a barnacle along the waterline of some grounded and rusted hull of a ghostship. And Phyllis, serene, slightly aloof, encouraging, but always, always just out of reach. My brother Carl's face was a death mask, unreadable, just as it had been in life.

Who am I?

After Carl's death I had stepped back from life, withdrawing into a shell, losing touch with my world, Key West, which apart from those two years in Korea was the only world I'd known. With Carl's death, it was as if ice tongs had suddenly been clamped to my heart, and I lived in some nameless region where it seemed that fear and dread would be with me all the days of my life.

Who am I?

Biking south toward the ocean I gazed at the sky on my way home. The trees along the dark, deserted street cast fragmented shadows as I made my way beneath the stars, guided by Venus while circumnavigating the potholed street.

"Don't fuck with me, Pop!" a voice said. I heard the swish of tires from another biker and felt a hand reach out and shove me as he went past. I tumbled, hearing the skid of rubber as the young rider braked his bike. Swerving back, he was on top of me when I hit the ground, leaning with his knee in my neck, pinning my arm as he searched my pockets with his free hand. He stripped my wallet of cash and was gone as quickly and silently as he'd arrived.

I'd landed on my left shoulder on the curb and lay there in the gutter for a moment stunned before getting to my feet, moving my arm to make sure nothing was broken, then retrieving the wallet minus its cash. There'd been twenty-five, thirty dollars in it. Enough to feed the kid's crack habit for a few hours. I felt nothing about the loss of the money. But *Pop!* And the fall from a bicycle was an assault on dignity.

I dusted my trousers, picked up the bike, and rode home, chaining the bike to a column on the front porch. I let myself in, turned on a light as Tom came out from his desk drawer to greet me, looking up at me as if I were a stranger.

In one evening I'd gone from high to low, playing for Asia and then being mugged. I took off my shirt and sat at the desk, massaging my shoulder and thinking of the pleasure a soothing shot of rum would provide right now. Casey had said there would be times like these for the rest of my life. But she wasn't here to provide the antidote, to talk me through it. I was on my own now, baby. I needed a distraction. I thought of calling Peggy, my ex-wife, but at three o'clock in the morning neither she nor her husband would have been in a receptive mood. I thought of other people I could call, but there was too much distance now, my life too remote.

I knew it was useless to go to bed. I went into the kitchen and stood in the dark, gazing into the lighted refrigerator, hoping for an answer. It wasn't there. I made a pot of coffee and sat up most of the night, drinking it.

21.

It was nearly five o'clock in the morning when I dropped into bed, exhausted but too wired from all the coffee and my thoughts to fall asleep. I picked up a book and tried to read, and later when I got up to pee, the wall clock in the kitchen showed six o'clock. Gray light was creeping in the east windows of the kitchen. I said to hell with it, put on a pair of swimming trunks and a T-shirt, and carried a towel and a pair of goggles down to the pier for an early-morning swim as I tried to shake off the jagged edge of caffeine-induced tension and insomnia.

I swam a mile, and by the time I came out the sun was well above the horizon. I walked back to the house, showered, shaved, fed Tom, and then lay down expecting only to rest for a few minutes. It was ten o'clock when I awoke.

After dressing, I squeezed half a lemon into a tall glass of water, thought about coffee and rejected it. Instead, I fried some bacon and scrambled three eggs, poured some Key West salsa over the eggs, and by noon I was ready to face the world.

The coroner, Wes Hutton, phoned just as I was finishing the dishes. "I'm interested in the Frank Maguire death," I told him.

"Yeah, Bud, it's one for the books all right."

"George said you weren't sure if it was suicide."

"No, no. Whoever killed him wanted it to look that way, but it was clearly murder."

"And the time of death?"

"Around one o'clock in the morning, I'd say. Give or take an hour or so."

"How about the autopsy. You turn up anything unusual?"

80

"Well, there was one thing. From the looks of Maguire's body I'd say he'd been in a fight not long before he was shot. There was evidence of bruising, the kind of lividity I'd associate with a fistfight."

"How bad was it?"

"Not serious enough to kill him, if that's what you mean. But he would have woke up in the morning feeling some aches and pains."

"Can you pinpoint when he might have been fighting in relation to the time of death?"

"Best guess, a couple of hours before he was shot."

"So sometime between eleven and midnight."

"Approximate. I'd have a hard time defending that in court, but between you and me I'd say, yes, a couple hours earlier at most."

I thanked Wes and hung up feeling troubled. Unless Frank had left the Hemingway House sometime after the party, returning later, which seemed unlikely, he would have been in the fight there if Wes Hutton's times were accurate.

I remembered Maguire's posturing, his belligerent attitude. He'd been drinking heavily, apparently feeling the macho spirit of his mentor, whose posthumous literary work Frank had undertaken to complete. Had he pushed himself into a corner, had to fight his way out, before being killed by the same person? But what difference did it make anyway? I was done with this case. It was now simply a nagging memory.

After weeks of putting off repairs to the house, I got out the cans of paint I'd purchased the other day and decided to spend the afternoon putting a coat of paint on the front of my office. A high-pressure ridge had moved in, replacing the damp mush we were accustomed to in July with some unusually drier air, perfect for painting. Of course within a day or two, when the humidity returned, we would only feel betrayed. I hosed down the outside of the building and waited for it to dry. Around two o'clock I was about ready to begin painting when I heard a distant clamor, some shouting, and turning to look down Duval Street, I saw a crowd of a hundred or more people a couple of blocks away in the street near the pier.

Two cops on motorcycles provided an escort as the mob began to march in my direction, some on bicycles, others on foot waving handmade placards and banners, and chanting, "No offshore oil. No offshore oil."

It was the protest march I'd read about a few days ago and forgotten. The placards showed oil wells surrounded by a circle with a red line drawn diagonally across them. As the protesters went by, I could see that they represented a good cross section of the community. Young hippies marching beside chamber-of-commerce types, and some of my people, older Conchs who would normally not have been caught dead in a protest march.

I put the paint away, closed up the house, and followed the demonstration on my bicycle. We worked our way down Duval Street, picking up additional support and steam as we went, until by the time we'd reached lower Duval and had crossed back to Mallory Square in front of the convention center, I estimated we were five hundred or more strong.

At three o'clock in the convention center a state legislative task force was scheduled to hold a public hearing with oil executives and lobbyists on both sides of the issue before making a final recommendation with regard to the leases the oil companies held in nearby waters.

I moved around the crowd, pausing to talk to people here and there. Among them I saw my ex-wife Peggy, whom I hadn't seen since Carl's funeral. She reminded me of that when I stopped to say hello.

"I've been lying low," I said. Normally, I had coffee with her once or twice a month, out of habit. Peggy had been close with my family, especially my mother.

"Bud, are you okay?" I listened to the genuine concern in her voice. She seemed to have grown thicker around the waist, the flesh of her face beginning to sag, and her frumpy clothing did nothing to enhance her appearance. In my mind I saw Asia standing again in my office, sexy in her baggy shorts.

"I'm fine," I said. Peggy and I had gone to school together, married when I returned from Korea, a marriage that lasted nearly ten years until my drinking and lack of interest in having children forced her elsewhere. It seemed so long ago, but in a curious way we had maintained an attachment.

"God," Peggy said, looking over the crowd, "this would have pleased Carl so much."

I smiled. "Yes, I suppose it would." It was hard to imagine Carl on the side of these demonstrators since he had been aligned for so many years with big money as represented by the oil barons and politicians who were now beginning to go into the convention center. But it was Peggy's nature never to find fault, and certainly not with the dead.

I saw Carl's protégé, Ira Holloway, the young senator who had been appointed by the governor to fill out the remainder of Carl's term until the fall elections. He even looked somewhat like a younger version of Carl, I thought. I started to move away from Peggy.

"Bud," she said, "please stay in touch."

I said I would and walked toward the red-brick building where the hearing was being held. I had caught sight of someone else I wanted to talk to. Ben Kantor was going inside, deep in conversation with another man whose back was to me. I followed, jostled by the crowd that was filing inside the hall, lost sight of Ben, and wound up wandering around the cavernous interior looking for him. I didn't see him, but the man Kantor had been talking to was up on the platform stage, talking now to Senator Holloway, who was on the task force. I watched the man next to Holloway leave the stage as the proceedings were about to start. I wouldn't have recognized him except that my conversation with Ben Kantor yesterday had provided a description.

Mickey Freeman was unmistakable in his Western suit, bolo tie, and cowboy boots.

22.

I listened for twenty minutes as the members of the task force introduced themselves, stated their concerns and goals, then proceeded to call on the individuals in the audience who had signed up to speak. The crowd continued to wave their placards, booing and hissing anyone who showed signs of support for drilling, and cheering those who didn't.

I watched the guys in the shirts and ties, their sleeves rolled up, make notes, ask questions, and fiddle with their glasses. There were ten of them onstage, considerably outnumbered by a mob, most of whom were dressed in shorts and T-shirts. The bias of the shirts and ties came through often enough to the displeasure of the shorts and T-shirts, but despite the mismatch of numbers, I had seen this sort of thing played out often enough to know the odds were in favor of the shirts and ties. Whatever they decided.

I went home and got a coat of paint on the front of the building, cleaned everything up, and at seven went over to the Cuban restaurant and ate a *palomilla* steak and french fries before going over to the Pier House and a crowd who'd come hoping for another night with Asia. They were disappointed.

When I finished at two o'clock in the morning, I kept to the lighted streets and rode by the Casa Marina where I stopped on impulse to see if Asia had left. A few late-night revelers still paraded through the grand lobby of the Casa with an occasional explosion of laughter coming from the adjoining bar. At the desk I learned that Asia had checked out a day ago, the previous night. It would have to have been late since she left the

84

Pier House sometime around ten.

I found a concierge taking a breather, seated beside one of the large potted areca palms inside the main door. He wore khaki shorts with knee-length white socks and a nameplate over the pocket of his tunic shirt.

"Were you on this same shift last night, Rob?" I asked.

He snapped up from his fold-up chair. "Yes, sir, Cap. Came on at eight o'clock. What can I do for you?"

I held a twenty folded lengthwise between my fingers. "You know Asia?"

"Not the way I'd like to." Rob grinned.

"But you'd recognize her."

"Hey, she lived here for a week."

"I hear she checked out last night. You might have helped her."

"Right on both counts."

"What time would that have been?"

"Somewhere after midnight, not long before my lunch break."

"Tell me about it."

"Nothing to tell. Loaded her bags in the trunk of a cab and watched her disappear into the night."

"You get where she was going?"

Rob looked at the twenty. "The airport."

I shook my head. "There aren't any flights out of here after ten o'clock."

"Hey, Cap, it's not my job to dispute destinations with our guests."

"You talk pretty good."

"College." Rob grinned again. "I'm in graduate school."

I held out my fist and the twenty disappeared almost with a sleight of hand, into Rob's pocket. "To higher education."

"You got it, Cap." He held the door for me as I went out.

I went home and got the Buick and drove along the beach road to the airport, no more than five minutes from the Casa

Marina. I parked at the curb and went inside the terminal, checking the departure boards behind the three airline counters. Just as I thought, the last flight had departed at ten. The next flight out would be at six this morning, less than four hours from now.

The terminal was empty so I walked into the lounge next door. Music blared from hidden speakers while a silent baseball game was being played on a large screen looming over the bar. I got the bartender's attention and shouted for a club soda. When he brought it, I gave him a couple bucks and tried to ask him about any late flights out of here. He ignored me and moved off.

Someone tapped me on the shoulder and I turned around to face Ray Quinn, a security guard who'd worked the airport for about as long as security guards had been out here.

"Bud, what the hell you doin' here this time of night? I heard you was on the wagon."

I held up my glass. "Soda. I'm checking some late-night flights."

"Wait a minute." Ray muscled his way up to the bar and got a Styrofoam cup of coffee. "Let's go outside."

I followed him back out to the terminal where it was quiet. Ray was my age, we'd gone to school together, but he seemed to have aged considerably since the last time I'd seen him. He pushed a finger in his ear and withdrew it. "How they sit in there for hours and not come out deaf I don't know. What was you saying to me?"

"I'm trying to find out about any late flights that might have gone out of here sometime after midnight last night."

"Might have been some private stuff go out. Nothing commercial."

"How could I find out about the privates?"

Ray smiled. "Best way is to ask. The tower shuts down at midnight so they would have records up until then, after that the Navy air station at Boca Chica takes over. The controllers have all gone home so unless it's important, you're going to have to wait till morning to get the flight records."

"It's important."

Ray sighed. "I can call the chief at home, wake him up, but he ain't going to like it."

I walked with Ray to the far end of the terminal where he had a cubbyhole of an office with a desk and a phone. He set his coffee on the desk and reached for the phone. I stood leaning against the doorway. I overheard Ray say that it was an official inquiry, and a few minutes later he hung up.

"There was a small private jet that went out of here last night about twelve-thirty. A pilot and one passenger."

"Where were they going?"

"New York."

"I wonder who owned the plane."

"Can't help you there. Be on record someplace, I'm sure. You'll be able to dig it up in the morning."

"You've been a big help, Ray. I owe you one."

"Nada. We're Conchs. One of them endangered species. We gotta stick together."

I clapped him on the back, walked out to the Buick, and drove home and went to bed. An endangered species. I'd never thought of myself that way, but I suppose Ray was right.

23.

George Lewis was seated alone at a table at the drugstore the next morning when I went in for breakfast. He motioned for me to join him.

"What gets you out this time of day?" I asked.

"You do." George looked unhappy, as if he'd gotten out of bed not long ago without enough sleep. I knew how he felt.

"I warned you, Bud." He pointed a stubby finger at me. He was a stocky man with thick, dark hair that had been wetted and combed down except for some loose strands in back that refused to be tamed.

"Warned me about what?" The waitress brought my coffee.

"Leveling with me."

I doctored the coffee. "I was protecting a client's right to privacy."

George leaned across the table. "Who happens to be the wife of a murder victim."

"Which doesn't restrict her right to privacy any more than anyone else's."

"Under the circumstances, Bud, I think it might."

"What circumstances?"

"Rumors are going around that she was down here looking for her husband. She wanted a divorce. And you were hired to find him."

"So what's the problem? It can get a little sordid sometimes, but it's honest enough work."

"She showed up at the Hemingway House the other night."

I felt some inner turmoil, the kind that was going to make it difficult to digest breakfast. "Asia?"

"Asia."

"Well, it was a party open to the public, right?"

"Don't play the wise guy with me, Bud. She was there. She was seen with Maguire. She was seen arguing with him."

"Says who?"

"Says me, goddamn it!" George leaned back, tilting his chair and jamming his thumbs in his waistband. He was breathing hard. When he had calmed down, George said, "Bud, you know what that place grosses in a week? I'll tell you. More than I make every month. Now you think they're not putting some pressure on me to get this solved so the place can reopen, then think again. I've got an investigation here and I don't have time to dick around with you."

"What do you want to know?"

"Where is she?"

"I don't know."

"Goddamn it, Bud, she's your fuckin' client."

"Not anymore she isn't. The case is closed. My job's done."

George nodded, a tic pulling at the corner of his left eye. He sat upright again. "We're talking to Sweetwater. We'll probably take him in later today for questioning."

I looked around for Sweets as if this were a joke. He wasn't at his usual place at the counter. "Now what do you want to do that for, George?"

George grinned, apparently satisfied that he'd finally riled me. "He was there the other night, too. Seems he got into a little boxing match with Maguire after hours. Not long before Maguire was killed. We've got to cover all the angles, Bud. You know how this business works."

"Maguire was shot."

"Yeah and guess what. The gun that shot him came from the Hemingway collection."

"It came out of the house?"

"It was in storage in a room below the director's office near where the fighters changed. Sweetwater had access."

My mother had frequently visited Hemingway's wife Pauline in the forties, and I had accompanied her once or twice when the Hemingway boys were there. Still, I don't have any clear memory of what was in the house. I know that Phyllis thought that once it was sold most of the family possessions were taken, and by the time it became a museum, the furnishings were simply an attempt to re-create the atmosphere of the place. Whether Hemingway would even have had a shotgun in Key West was arguable, but one might have been added given the part they played in Hemingway's life.

"Was the room locked?"

"No. Anyone could have gone in there. In fact it was used that night as a dressing room for the fighters."

"The gun was loaded?"

"There was a box of shells in the case with it. Whoever did it knew where it was and forced open the gun case."

"It's just a process of narrowing down suspects then."

"Beginning with Sweetwater. Here's a possible scenario. Maguire was a Hemingway nut. He wants the firsthand experience of mixing it up with someone who'd fought him. Sweetwater could have decked him."

"Sweets is eighty years old."

"And strong as an ox."

"You're accusing Sweets of murder?"

"Not accusing anybody of anything. Just trying to work up some possibilities. See what you think of them."

"I don't think much of them."

"I didn't think you would. You knew Sweets was in the ring with Maguire though, didn't you?"

I didn't say anything.

"Look, there was enough left of Maguire's face to determine that he'd been belted shortly before he was killed. It stands to reason."

George was silent for a moment. "The thing is, we find out that's the way it happened and you knew about it, it puts you in an awkward position." We stared at one another. George stood up. "You get a change of attitude, maybe we can work something out."

George left. The waitress came to the table to take my order. I told her I wasn't hungry. Coffee only this morning. She looked at me as if I were sick. And I was.

Back home I put a call through to the manager of the airport. When he came on the line, I told him I was interested in a private plane that had gone out a couple nights ago about twelve-thirty in the morning bound for New York.

"Yeah, you're the second person interested in that plane." The other one, I would have been willing to bet, was George Lewis. I listened to the information that came across the line.

The plane that had flown out that night with Asia on it was destined for New York. It was leased by a consortium of companies in the entertainment industry, as well as Globe Oil.

I got on my bike, rode over to the courthouse, and went up to Judge Watson's office on the second floor. Phyllis had always referred to him as Just because of his judicial integrity, and the nickname had stuck. Just had married one of Captain Billy's many cousins, a marriage that ended in tragedy when his young wife and unborn child were killed in a car accident. It had left Just a recluse, his only interest in life his profession and fishing.

Just was about to go into court. "I've got ten minutes. Come in here." An unlit cigar was clamped in Just's mouth. "Bud, how do you?"

We sat down at a long conference table cluttered with papers. Just was in his sixties, tall, thin, with a thick head of hair that was mostly gray now. He pushed a hand through it.

"I'm fine," I said. "I came about Sweetwater."

"What about him?"

"He's being held and questioned about the murder at the Hemingway House the other night."

"He charged with anything?"

"I don't think so."

Just nodded. "They can hold him for twenty-four hours without bringing charges. After that they've got to let him go."

"I want to talk to him."

"He have a lawyer?"

"I doubt it."

Just thought for a moment. "If he's charged and can't afford his own attorney, the court will appoint someone from the public defender's office to represent him. You want to get to see him right away, you'd be better off finding him a lawyer."

"Who would you recommend?"

Just leaned his head against the back of the chair. After a moment he pushed the chair back and reached for the phone on the desk behind him. "Get me Will Clark," Just said into the receiver, then held it to his ear while he continued to roll the cigar in his mouth. Seconds later he said, "Will, can you come up here? I've got something you might be interested in." Just hung up.

"Will Clark's young," Just said to me. "He's recently gone into practice on his own. I've got a good feeling about him. Where have they got Sweetwater?"

"I assume here at the jail."

Just picked up the phone again and called down to the jail. He asked about Sweetwater, listened for a while, then said that a lawyer was coming down to talk to Sweetwater and the judge would appreciate their cooperation.

Five minutes later I shook hands with Will Clark, and together we took the stairs down to the holding cell where Sweetwater had been brought.

24.

The cubicle was windowless with concrete walls painted pea green. A metal desk and two straight-backed chairs were all the furnishings in the room. A wire cage surrounded a bare light bulb in the ceiling. Sweetwater sat on one of the chairs, his body erect, defiant, when a sheriff's deputy opened the door to let us in.

Sweets stared at me, shaking his head. "Bud, isn't this something?"

I introduced him to Will Clark, and the two of them shook hands. "I can't afford no lawyer."

"I know that, Sweets. Don't worry about it." I sat down in the chair opposite, a few feet away from him. Clark perched on the desk. "I've got to ask you some questions," I said.

"I'm gettin' good at answerin' questions." Sweets forced a grin.

"Why didn't you tell me about the fight you had with Maguire?" I asked.

Sweetwater looked at his hands, rubbing his knuckles. "It a joke, Bud. The man's idea."

"Maguire? "

Sweets nodded. "I thought I'd best not say anything to anyone when I heard what happened."

"Tell us what did happen."

"Maguire want to know all about my time around here in the old days, askin' me all kinds of questions. Then he suggest we go a round like I did with Papa. Shit, how I know he got a glass jaw?"

93

"You knocked Maguire out?"

"Barely tapped him. The man go down like a sack of concrete."

I should have known Frank would be working right up to the end. "Do you remember what time it was when all this happened?"

"The fights ended 'bout ten o'clock. I had stuff to do and talkin' to different people afterwards. Sometime round ten-thirty I reckon I talked to Maguire."

"When did you get in the ring?"

"Don't know. We talked for about an hour."

"Was there anyone still around then?"

"Nah, everybody gone, I guess. I didn't see no one anyway."

"No one even with Maguire?"

Sweets shook his head.

"How did he seem?"

"Seem okay. Interested. Writin' stuff down in a notebook."

"So when you boxed with him it must have been close to midnight?"

"Probably."

Wes Hutton had said he thought Maguire was killed sometime between midnight and two A.M.

"What happened when Maguire went down?"

Sweets shook his head. "I got the salts, took the gloves off him, and he walked away."

"He didn't say anything?"

"What he gonna say? Be embarrassed, I think."

"But he was okay, he wasn't angry with you?"

"Seem a little groggy. Nothing serious."

"You didn't see where he went."

"No, Bud. I was tired. I got out of there myself. Went home and went to bed."

"But someone must have seen you because George Lewis heard about it."

Sweets shrugged.

"I want you to think about that. Try to remember who might have been around."

"Some of the staff maybe. I don't know. I appreciate you bein' in my corner on this, Bud."

I nodded.

"Make me feel a whole lot better."

I wasn't sure how it made me feel, especially with the information Sweetwater had just given me.

"Wes Hutton, the coroner, found marks on Maguire. You must have hit him pretty good."

"I punched him a few times, body punches. We be playin' around, he wanting me to show him Papa's style, and he walked into one. The man got a glass jaw. I told you that, Bud."

Will Clark coughed and stood up. "Why didn't you volunteer this information to George Lewis when you heard Maguire had been killed?" Will asked.

Sweets continued to look at me. "The man dead. Who you think gonna believe an old black man? Not George Lewis."

"I believe you, Sweets. And anybody in this town who knows you will believe you."

"George Lewis ain't gonna believe me."

"He's just doing his job. You'll be out of here soon. Times are different now, Sweets."

"Ain't nothin' different about them far as the law concerned. You got some color in your skin and you hurt a white boy, you in big trouble."

I felt the downward spiral of time, the years compressing, and with it a certain remorse in the knowledge that what Sweetwater said was true.

"Tell me what happened after you hit Maguire," Will said.

"I went to get the salts."

"Where?"

"In a storage room below Miss Clampitt's office."

"Was the place unlocked?"

"It had been all night."

"Then what happened?"

"I brought the man around."

"How long did that take?"

"Couple minutes. I don't know. I talk to him for a while. He okay. Groggy, like I said."

"But he wasn't mad at you? And you didn't get mad at him at any time, did you?"

"No, sir. We joke a little bit and he wander off."

"You're sure you didn't see where he went?"

Sweets shook his head. I looked at Will.

Sweets kept looking at me as if I'd asked the question.

"When did you leave?" Will asked.

"Soon as I put the stuff from the fights away and close up the storage."

"Did you go out the front?"

"Yeah, walked right out the front gate."

"Was anybody around there?" Will said.

"Somebody in the house, the light on, but I didn't see them."

Will nodded. "You remember what time it was?"

Sweetwater shook his head. "Round midnight when I got home, that's all I know."

Sweetwater's wife had died several years ago and he now lived alone. I was aware that he had many friends and relatives in town who looked after him. People who would give him support now, but beyond myself and the judge I couldn't think of anyone else who could help him out of here, at least until charges had been filed and bond set.

I tried to assure him that everything would be all right. When we left, Sweetwater was seated rigid in his chair, staring straight back at me with dark, proud eyes.

25.

Yellow police tape surrounded the grounds of the Hemingway House. I found Ruth Clampitt in her office chain-smoking Salem Lights. "This is outrageous," Ruth said when I went in. "Do you know how much money we're losing?"

"More than the chief of detectives makes in a month." I smiled.

Ruth looked at me oddly through the thick lenses of her sequined glasses. "It isn't funny. Particularly this week of all weeks."

"Were you here all evening the night Maguire was killed?"

"I was here early but I had a dinner engagement. I came back at eleven o'clock. The fight was finished and people had left except for some of the staff."

"Who was that?"

"Let's see. Wallace Stevens was here, the guy on the front gate."

I remembered Wallace.

"And Liz Evans, my assistant. They were closing up. Oh, and I saw the guy who refereed the fights."

"That was all? No stragglers from the public?"

"Not that I saw, but I didn't really look around when I saw Liz here. I knew everything was in order." Ruth lit a cigarette.

"It's ironic. You were just here asking about Maguire the other day."

I nodded. "I suppose it's ironic, but the police are holding Sweetwater."

Ruth lit another cigarette. "Who is he?"

"The guy who is refereeing the fights here."

"He did it?" She didn't seem at all surprised.

"I'm sure that he didn't do it. But they're questioning him anyway. He was one of the last people to see Maguire alive."

Ruth took off her glasses, tapping the tip of one of the earpieces against her front tooth for a second before putting the glasses on her desk. "Well, then it's out of our hands."

"Not mine. I still have some questions."

She looked annoyed but didn't say anything.

"When you came back here after your dinner, you said that Wallace and Liz were closing up."

"That's right. They were getting rid of some of the litter. A cleanup crew came in early the next morning and finished going over the grounds. They found Maguire in the pool house."

"Did you speak to either Liz or Wallace when you arrived here?"

"I checked with Liz to make sure there were no problems. I didn't actually see Wallace, but Liz told me he was around."

"How did she seem?"

"Fine. Everything had gone off without a hitch."

"Do you know what time they finally left?"

"Sometime before midnight, I believe."

"It's a critical time. Is there a way of being more exact?"

"I can get Liz to come up if you want." She picked up the phone, pushed a button on the intercom, and a few seconds later Liz appeared. "You remember Gideon Lowry, don't you?" Ruth asked.

Liz smiled. "Of course." She came in and took a seat in front of the desk beside me, smiling brightly as though this were just a matter of routine.

"I was asking Ruth about the time you closed up the night of the murder. She said it was around midnight. Can you be more precise?"

"Well, I went to bed at twelve-fifteen because I remember

checking the alarm clock. I couldn't have been home more than half an hour."

"And Wallace?"

"Wallace was still here when I left, but I assume he was about ready to leave."

I looked at Ruth. "Is that normal, for Wallace to lock up?"

Ruth laughed. "He's been here for twenty years, longer than anyone, and if you asked Wallace, I'm sure he'd tell you he really runs the place."

"What sort of person is he?"

"Cranky," Liz said.

"But dependable," Ruth added.

Liz smiled and nodded. "He has a set of keys and is often the last to leave here when there's an event."

"Would he have been inside the house after you left?"

Liz looked perplexed for a moment. "No, there would have been no reason for him to be inside the house."

"Are the lights inside the house left on at night?"

"No, only the outside security lighting."

"When Sweetwater left here, also around midnight, he said someone was inside. The lights were on."

"That's odd," Liz replied. "I can't think of any reason for him to have gone in."

"I'd like to talk to him. I wonder if I could call him from here?"

Ruth handed the phone across to me and dialed a number from an address book she had opened.

When he answered, I told him where I was and said I would like to come by for minute. I had a couple of questions. He sounded reluctant to see me, but if I could make it over there ASAP, he said he would wait for me.

I was there in ten minutes.

26.

Wallace Stevens lived in a one-bedroom walk-through apartment on the second floor of a Conch house in need of paint. Gingerbread men decorated the railings around the porches, and a large almond tree in the front yard buried the house behind thick foliage. The hallways were dark and dusty, but Wallace's apartment was like a gauzy Victorian dream, with a canopy draped from the ceiling in a shiny material that billowed like a parachute. The walls, too, were covered with fabric, and the floor was highly polished hardwood. The furnishings seemed shabby, and more suited to a drawing room in one of the many old whorehouses that had existed in Key West in another era. I recognized the distantly familiar smell of booze, which hung like smoke in the air.

Something was incongruous here, some feminine aspect to the surroundings that was out of sync with Wallace's brooding, bearded presence. The barrel chest tapered down to slender hips. His head was large; the face, covered by the neatly trimmed gray beard, held some distant expression in the wide-set eyes. Barefoot, he had on jeans and a white shirt, the two top buttons open with a gold chain nestled in the gray chest hair.

"Well, I suppose you want to talk about the murder the other night." His voice, a thin reed of sound, almost timorous, surprised me once again.

"You were there until late I'm told. I thought you might have seen something."

Wallace dipped his head to one side. "I've been in that

place for twenty years. I've seen plenty." He sat down on the couch and put his feet up on a white wicker coffee table.

Uninvited, I sat down on an uncomfortable straight-backed chair opposite Wallace. "I was thinking more of the time of the murder."

Wallace shook his head. "Can't help you."

"What about Sweetwater, the guy who refereed the fights. Did you see him around?"

"I said I was the last person to leave. I didn't see anyone."

"Which doesn't mean someone wasn't there."

Wallace shrugged. "There are plenty of places to hide back there."

"Had you seen Frank Maguire, the guy who was killed?"

"Sure. A couple of times."

"Besides that night?"

"Yeah, that wasn't the first time he'd been around. He hung out there a lot."

I was surprised. "Doing what?"

"He came by the house once or twice, took the tour, then hung around to talk to me."

"What about?"

"The usual. The history of the house, its changes, my impressions of it over the years."

"Did he tell you why he was interested?"

"Another writer writing a book about the place."

"Another one. You get a lot of them?"

"Enough. But Maguire was different."

"In what way?"

"He was more interested in the business side of the place."

"And you were able to help him."

A thin smile spread across Wallace's face. "Somewhat. It's no secret the place is in trouble."

"Financially? "

"Ruth isn't the best of managers." Wallace paused, then added, "She's making a fortune, but it's all going into her own pocket."

"How bad's the trouble?"

"The house is for sale again."

"Any offers?"

"One. From a corporation."

"Don't tell me. Globe Oil."

"How'd you know? It's been a closely guarded secret."

"It's too small a town for closely guarded secrets. You know that. Word gets around."

Wallace became disgruntled, irritable, and began making catty remarks about Ruth Clampitt. When she took over the management of the house, according to Wallace, it became a business above all else. The magic went out of working there. There was less attention to the accuracy of the facts surrounding the house, and more to the details of getting busloads of Japanese tourists through the grounds as quickly as possible. At one time Wallace himself had conducted tours. He prided himself on relating little-known anecdotes of Hemingway's life in the house. Now that was all forgotten. Today, it was just a pat tour that anyone who'd memorized the script could have given.

When he was finished grumbling, I stood up to leave. "By the way, what were you doing inside the house just before you left that night?"

Wallace stared at me blankly. "Inside? I wasn't inside the house."

"People saw a light on in there. They thought it was you."

"Wrong. I never went inside the house that night."

I stared at him for a moment, again feeling some pity for a man living out his lonely life behind a mask, eased by alcohol.

I left and returned to the Hemingway House. People were taking pictures on the sidewalk outside. Liz stood behind the closed gate talking to an elderly couple in matching Bermuda shorts when I rode up. She let me in. "It's unbelievable. All anyone wants to know about is the murder."

"What are you telling them?"

"There's not much I can say. Word is out that the guy was a writer and that he was writing a book about Hemingway."

"That won't hurt business."

Liz smiled. "If we ever get back to business. I suppose it's rather sad."

I shrugged. Like death, the promotion of tourism didn't take holidays around here. It might be sad, but I was sure Ruth would find a way to capitalize on it, tastefully, of course. "I wonder if I could take a look at that storage area under Ruth's office?"

Liz looked at her watch. "I don't see why not."

I followed her around back and crossed the cobbled patio by the boxing ring. Liz pushed open an old wooden door that had been cut down to accommodate the less than full-size opening in the back of the building.

Inside it was dark and faintly musty, a smell of old sweat, the concrete floor gritty underfoot. Liz turned on a light, a bare bulb in a socket above the door. The room was small, no more than ten feet square, with plaster walls. "Is this where the fighters changed?"

"Yes. And over here is the storage room." She opened another door in the wall and we entered a larger room packed with boxes and various household furnishings.

"What is this stuff?"

"Junk. Some of it came out of the house, but a lot of it I think may have belonged to various employees over the years who stored it here and forgot about it."

"Is any of it legitimate?"

"You mean part of the Hemingway collection?"

I nodded.

"A few things in here were donations from people who had stuff from the period, but I doubt whether any of it actually belonged to the Hemingways."

I noticed the gun cabinet and went over to examine it.

There was a .22 single-shot rifle and an old 6.5 Mannlicher that would have brought down an elephant.

"That was in the house at one time, but Ruth decided to have it taken out when she came in. She didn't like the idea of guns in the house."

"And you don't think it was Hemingway's."

"I believe it was donated."

A box of dusty shotgun shells, twelve-gauge, was in a drawer. I picked one up and put it in my pocket.

"I didn't even know those were there," Liz said.

"Someone did. Is this door kept locked?"

"No, we lock the outside door, but not this one. No one ever comes back in here unless they're with staff."

"But that door was open last night when the fights were going on. Anyone could have come in here, taken something out, and it wouldn't have been missed. Right?"

"Yes, that's true."

We went outside. "Wallace said he wasn't in the house that night, never went in there."

"Oh, I'm sure he was lying. Wallace has always wanted to be a writer. He plays at it in the house sometimes."

"How do you know that?"

"Oh, I've caught him. He's always scribbling in notebooks. I know that he likes going in the house and hanging out when no one is around, probably hoping the muse will rub off on him. I wouldn't say anything to Ruth. I suppose he believes I don't know."

"How long have you known him?"

"Not too long. A year or two. He's been here much longer than I have. I think he told me twenty years."

"Do you think he might resent Ruth?"

Liz's simple face suddenly looked troubled. "What do you mean?"

"Maybe he thinks he should be running this place."

Liz thought about it for a minute. "I suppose it's possible.

Wallace is a bit eccentric."

I walked around to the back and stood near the entrance to the pool house, a distance of only a few yards, all camouflaged somewhat by shrubbery. A fence ran around the back side of the property, but with sufficient space between it and the outbuildings to allow passage. The fence would have been easy enough to get over if someone was trying to get out without using the front gate. And at night, with the lights turned out, this area would have been shrouded in darkness. Liz went back to the house.

I wandered around, looking at the ground, looking for anything and finding nothing. When I came back around to the pool house, I heard voices and looked through the shrubbery to see Ruth Clampitt standing near the back door to the main house. She was talking to Mickey Freeman. I stood quietly until they were finished and Mickey walked around to the front and Ruth returned to her office.

Then I left. Mickey was getting in a car parked in the lot across the street from the house. I got on my bike and followed it, with some luck of traffic and stoplights, to the nearby Casa Marina Hotel.

27.

"Afternoon, Cap. You gonna tether the steed or you just passing through?" Rob, the concierge whom I had spoken to the other night, stepped down from the curb of the semicircular drive at the entrance to the hotel.

"You work all shifts?"

"Just came on days this morning."

"The cowboy who just went in, is he staying here?"

"The tall Texan?" Rob drawled mockingly. "A real big spender, Cap. Just like you. Yeah, he hangs his hat here. Our people seem to be keeping you busy."

I hesitated, trying to decide whether to go in and have a word with Freeman or return to the Hemingway House and talk to Ruth Clampitt. "You know if he's checking out anytime soon?"

Rob grinned. "Well, that kind of information calls for some research."

I worked my wallet out of my khakis and flashed a ten.

"Be right with you, Cap."

I watched him disappear inside and a minute later come back out. "Nix on the departure. He's here through the end of the week."

I palmed the bill and shook hands with Rob. "Don't go to sleep on your post."

"Never. Always a pleasure doing business with you, Cap. Stop by any old time."

I rode back to the Hemingway House, getting there a few minutes before noon. Ruth Clampitt was just leaving.

106

"Do you have a minute?" I asked.

"Not really. I have a luncheon engagement."

"This won't take long." We were standing on the sidewalk in front of the house. Beneath the cool exterior, the painted smile, Ruth seemed anxious. "I didn't know you knew Mickey Freeman," I said.

Ruth reached up and fiddled with a strand of costume jewelry around her neck. "Mickey Freeman?" She looked contemplatively into the distance.

"The guy who was in your office half an hour ago."

"What's that got to do with your investigation? If you're going to hang around here, you'll see a lot of people coming in and out of my office."

"It may have a lot to do with it. I hear from Wallace that the place is for sale."

"I'm sorry I'm not at liberty to discuss the business of the Hemingway House with you."

"What about Frank Maguire?"

"What about him?"

"How well did you know him?"

"I didn't know him at all."

"Despite the fact that he spent time here, questioned the staff, and went through the house several times. He was researching a book. How did he miss you?"

Ruth sighed. "Oh, yes, he talked to me a couple of times. I can hardly say I knew him."

"Did you tell the police?"

"They didn't ask."

"Miss Clampitt, a man's being held and questioned about the murder of Frank Maguire. A man I've known all my life. He didn't kill Maguire. I'm trying to find out the truth of what happened here the other night. I need your cooperation."

Ruth stared at me for a moment. "I'll do what I can, but I won't compromise the business negotiations of this house. And I really must go. I'm already late."

Ruth turned and walked to the corner. I watched her cross the street, striding purposefully, a woman with a mission. She got in her car and drove off, and I bicycled home.

I was tired, hungry, and frustrated. A day of too many questions and too few answers. A couple of messages were on my answering machine, one from Ben Kantor, the other from Casey.

Not in a mood to talk about her new boyfriend, I delayed calling Casey. I sat down at my desk and looked at the mail. There were a couple of bills and some subscription advertising, the kind with different type and colored ink used to set off something so irresistible that it would change my life. I could count on one hand the things that had changed my life. None of them had anything to do with magazines. Still, out of distraction rather than hope, I read every word.

Then I called Kantor. "I've gone over Frank's material," he said.

"Anything of interest?"

"Yes. Mickey Freeman."

"I know. He wants to buy the Hemingway House."

"How do you know that?"

"A disgruntled employee over there."

"Do you know what the plans were?"

"No."

"Mickey was buying the house. Frank was going to live in it."

"What!"

"The Hemingway House was going to revert to a private home once more, with Frank Maguire the writer in residence."

"But why? I know Frank had an obsession with Hemingway, but isn't that a little extreme?"

"Not for Mickey Freeman, it wouldn't be."

"Because he was getting Frank off his back?" I thought of how Mickey Freeman had made Asia's career.

"There's that, and more. Mickey was making inroads into

exploring for oil in Cuba."

"How is that possible? We've got an embargo against Cuba."

"Globe has interests in companies outside the U.S., which could shield them."

"Isn't that risky?"

"American businesses are dying to get into Cuba. Other countries are already investing heavily there. You can be sure we're poised to go in as soon as Castro falls. Or the minute Washington changes its policy. Whichever comes first."

"So Freeman is just hedging his bets."

"Looks that way."

"And compromising Frank in the process."

Cuba was also Hemingway country, so it appeared that Frank Maguire had sold out. Mickey Freeman had found his Achilles' heel. Unless of course Frank wanted Mickey to think that he'd sold out—which could explain a lot. Even murder.

"What Frank was doing is richer than that," Kantor said. "He was working all of this right into the present."

I wasn't sure I understood. I asked Kantor if I could take a look at the material Frank had compiled.

"Sure, you want to pick it up, I'll be here."

I told him I would be right over.

28.

George Lewis's black sedan was parked on the sidewalk so as not to block the narrow street in front of the entrance to Ben Kantor's compound. I rang the bell on the outside gate. A cop opened it, seemed to recognize me, stepping back to let me in.

I walked along the pathway to the cottages and found George standing in the doorway to one of them. He turned when I came up on the porch.

Kantor was standing inside the hallway. "You again," Lewis said. "Bud, you aren't going to be a pain in the butt for me, are you?"

I shook my head and spoke to Kantor.

"You two know each other?" George asked.

"We met once," I said, "when I was looking for Maguire."

"Maguire had one of the guesthouses here, but there's nothing in it except for a few clothes," George said. "The guy's turning into a real mystery man. He's living here but nobody knows anything about him."

"He was writing a book," Kantor said.

"Yeah, you told me. About Hemingway. Where is it?"

I shot Kantor a look. He just shrugged. "Maybe he sent it to his publisher already."

"Who would that be?"

"I don't know," Ben said.

"See what I mean," George said, turning to me. "Now I've got to go and track his wife down, some pop star he hadn't been living with but who hired you to find him so she could get a divorce. Except now she's disappeared. Peculiar, ain't it?"

110

"Very peculiar," I said.

George shook his head and stepped back in the hallway.

"Either of you guys remember something, anything, about Maguire, please give me a call." His voice had turned sarcastic. Then he went out the door.

"You showed up at the right time," Kantor said. "I wasn't going to say anything about Maguire's other writing until you'd seen it, but he was pushing."

"There's nothing in there that will make any difference to the police in the next twenty-four hours, is there?"

"I doubt it, but I don't want it to come back on me."

"Don't worry. I can handle George. What happened to the Hemingway book Frank was writing?"

"I returned it to Jocelyn."

"Is she here?"

"Until the end of the week when she leaves for Mexico."

"Where can I find her?"

Kantor disappeared and came back a moment later with several notebooks and Jocelyn's address written out on a card.

"You know that *Rolling Stone*'s sending a reporter down here. Aren't they going to be interested in this?"

"Probably, but if you can take care of the police, I'll handle the press." Kantor smiled. "Enjoy your reading."

George Lewis was sitting in the sedan, worrying a toothpick back and forth across his lips when I came out. The cop who'd been with him was gone. George flagged me over. I leaned down, resting my hands on the open window.

"What's in the notebooks?"

"Some personal records for my client."

"What client?"

"Asia."

"I thought you said she wasn't your client any longer, that case was closed."

"This is the final settlement."

"Anything that bears on this case that I should look at?"

"Nope."

George regarded me with evil intensity. "Bud, I can subpoena that faster than you can whistle Dixie. Keep that in mind."

"I'll do that."

George pulled the toothpick from his mouth and flicked it past me out the window. "So how do you figure this?"

"I don't figure it. I'm as lost as you are."

Lewis looked at me as if I'd insulted him. "I doubt that."

I shrugged.

George stared back out the windshield, one arm resting on the back of the seat. "A guy comes to Key West, holes up in a compound while writing a book about Hemingway. He keeps to himself until his wife shows up and hires you to find him, then he goes to the fights one night and talks to Sweetwater before getting himself knocked off in the pool house of the Hemingway House." George shook his head. "What's missing in this picture?"

"A motive I suppose."

George nodded. "What about the wife? She wants a divorce. He doesn't want to give it to her so she blows him away. Happens all the time. You talked to your nonclient, Asia?"

"Not recently."

"Neither have we, but we found out she flew out of here the other night on a private plane. Did you know that?"

"I knew it."

"But you didn't want to say anything?"

"I didn't know it when I saw you last," I lied.

"Bud, you're a pistol. Do me a favor, will you?"

"What's that?"

"Don't play games with me on this one. I don't want to have to come to you with a pry bar to get information. It will be too painful. For you."

I stood back from the car and saluted. "Take it easy,

George. You do your job and I'll do mine. We'll get to the bottom of this."

George lifted two fingers before snapping over the ignition. I got on my bike and pedaled home.

29.

There was no directory listing for Asia in New York. An operator gave me the number for an MTV recording studio in Manhattan. When I called that number, I got through to a receptionist who put me on hold to listen to what sounded like a recording of MTV music while I waited for the director. I held the phone away from my ear, barely hearing the next woman who came on the line. I told her I was trying to reach Asia. I told her it was urgent. Another interlude with recorded music before she came back and said Asia wasn't in yet, but she would be glad to take a message. I left my name and number.

Two hours later the phone rang. It was Asia. "Gideon, what is it? Your message said it was urgent." She didn't sound like a woman running away from murder.

"I need to ask you some questions. The police are looking for you now."

"You told them about me?"

"I didn't have to, Asia. They're investigating a murder. I told you they were going to want to question you."

"Will you represent me? Can't I hire you to handle it? Do this one thing for me, Gideon. Please."

"It doesn't work that way. There aren't a lot of leads and they want to talk to anyone who had any connection with Frank. Especially someone who might have benefited by his death."

"What do you mean?"

"You showed up at the Hemingway House and talked to Frank the same night he was killed."

"Who told you such a thing?"

"Please, Asia. Don't deny it. You were seen."

In a whimpering voice, she said, "I couldn't help it. He called me. He demanded I come."

"Who called you?"

"Frank. It must have been after you talked to him."

"What did he want?"

"He wanted to see me. He tried to talk me out of the divorce. He said he was going to be living there. We could both live there."

"Where? At the Hemingway House?"

"Yes. I thought he was crazy."

"He didn't tell you that your old friend Mickey Freeman was buying it for him?"

"No, Frank didn't mention Mickey."

"And neither did you."

"What do you mean?"

"You flew out of here on a private plane."

"Yes, I got word that the plane was available and so I took it."

"Word from whom?"

"My manager."

"Do you know who owns the plane?"

"It's on lease to several companies including MTV."

"Do you know who else?"

"No. Should I?"

"Globe Oil and Mickey Freeman."

There was a long pause.

"Oh, God. How bad is it?"

"Bad enough that I think you should come back down here, go to the police, and talk to them. Don't make them come to you."

"I have work. We're on a tight schedule. This is such bad timing." She sounded bitter, even angry. "Can't we delay this?"

"It's only advice. Take it or leave it." I let her think about it.

"Oh, Gideon, once my name's dragged into this there will

be a lot of bad publicity." From her choked voice, I guessed that now Asia was trying to hold back the tears. Something in me wanted her to cry, as if her tears could validate her emotions, but I knew she was enough of an actress to fake even that. I told her I would help her but she should be here. She agreed to come back but not until the recording sessions were finished. It might be a day or two. Before hanging up she also said that she would contact George Lewis.

Even though I felt an acute sense of dissatisfaction, there seemed nothing more I could do for Asia. I tried to put her out of my mind, to forget about this strange femme fatale with the grainy voice and the emotional balance of a teenager; to forget the painted toes and the shaved pubes. She wore her disguises with the unpredictability of a tropical summer storm. To hell with her. She was too complicated for me and I shut her out completely and totally for a couple of hours.

I missed Casey, missed her more than I would have thought possible, the missing sweetened perhaps by the knowledge that she was now with someone else. We had never cemented our connection, both of us comfortable in the unarticulated, and nonbinding, aspect of that relationship. We were friends who sometimes slept together, which seemed to suit both our temperaments, although I was aware that she, more than I, would probably want something more decisive sooner or later.

Casey's focus in the years that we hung out together was sobriety, while I was still having an affair with alcohol. It was ironic that at the time I made the decision to get sober, Casey decided to leave Key West. Not that I believed my not drinking would have changed our personal status in any way, but sober I felt more responsible, more inclined to take seriously something that I had for years only taken for granted. The bigger irony of course was that for me getting sober was a personal commitment, one that had required no group support role, and while it had been less than six months since I'd had a drink, I was confident that I would never drink again. Casey, on the other hand, relied on the resources and affirmation of others to maintain her equilibrium, but after leaving her support group here, venturing into the larger world, she confided in me that she felt more threatened of slipping than she had in all the time she was here dealing with me when I was drinking.

Neither of us would ever know what was lost by our individual decisions, but the fact that I felt the loss seemed to me enough.

Like me, Casey was provincial, and like my mother, Phyllis, had migrated here from a small Southern town in Virginia—although I never made too much of that particular coincidence because there was nothing else in their characters that appeared to overlap.

Phyllis had spent her life in a union with my father, a man I judged unsuited to her character; though in many respects Casey and I were more compatible than my parents, I'm sure she had never seen me as a man to whom she would have devoted her life, and by the time I'd reached a point when I might again think of commitment, it was too late. Casey was gone.

I tried to forget both Asia and Casey by seeking out another woman, one with a different set of problems, including a Hemingway manuscript.

30.

Jocelyn Beatty sat on the balcony of her time-share over-looking Key West harbor, her legs outstretched, her feet resting on the balcony railing. She was petite, not quite delicate, but there was a hardness in her eyes that I hadn't seen there the last time we met; eyes that were gray as ash and fixed on me like laser beams.

"I've known Frank about ten years," Jocelyn said in answer to my question. "We met in California at a book signing when he published the Hemingway book."

"Were you close?"

Her eyes dug in a little deeper until I shifted my gaze, looking down to the water where a powerboat planed across the harbor, its bow jutting from the water, a rooster tail of water flying in its wake.

"You mean was I sleeping with him?"

"I didn't say that."

"And I didn't say you did. I just wondered what you meant by 'close.'"

"Let's let it mean whatever you want it to mean." I turned back to her. She smiled. It was a tight, controlled smile that was as cold as a knife in the back.

"I liked him. Even though he was getting a little carried away lately. I think he saw himself as the heir to the Hemingway throne. But then he isn't the first American writer to go through that phase."

"I understand he was working on an unfinished manuscript of Hemingway's that you own."

"It wasn't something we were advertising. It is a partial manuscript of a novel about Key West and Cuba and the making of a movie of a writer's novel."

"How did you happen to get possession of it?"

Jocelyn tossed her head, sending the trademark solitary dangling earring dancing. "What is this? An interrogation?"

"For the moment it's curiosity." I gave her my warmest smile.

"I married into the Hemingway family. Surely by now you know that."

"I knew it, and I also know you divorced out of it. None of which explains the manuscript."

"It was part of the settlement. My husband signed it over to me. There are plenty of scraps of Hemingway writing still around. I thought this was salvageable with the right writer."

"Which is why you chose Frank?"

"More because I thought he could write it and keep the original spirit and intent intact." Jocelyn sounded annoyed. I tried not to let it bother me.

"What would a book like this have done for him?"

Jocelyn shrugged. "Who can say? But his name would have been linked to Hemingway's forever."

"Frank didn't finish it then."

"No, the book is about two-thirds done."

"What happens now?"

"I find someone else to do it."

"Any candidates?"

"Maybe Nick Farr. He's not the writer Frank was, but I think he can finish it."

"Did Frank say anything to you about moving into the Hemingway House?"

Jocelyn smiled. "No, he didn't mention it. It would have been a little crowded, wouldn't it, with all the tourists going through there?"

"There's a rumor circulating that a guy by the name of

Mickey Freeman was negotiating to buy it."

"I've never heard of Mickey Freeman."

"He's the head honcho at Globe Oil. He's down here because of this task force that's considering renewing the offshore oil leases. Frank had written about Globe some years ago when he was out in California. Mickey got Frank's wife started in the music business. Probably as a way of trying to neutralize Frank. The theory is he was trying to do it again by buying the house and installing Frank in it."

"A rather expensive bribe, isn't it? Was he going to close it down to tourists?"

I shrugged. "I don't know the details. Maybe Frank was going to be part of the tour." A replacement for Wallace Stevens, I thought.

Jocelyn laughed. "Yes, I can see it would have been a place where Frank could have created his own myth."

"Or expanded on someone else's."

"But what's any of that got to do with Frank's death?"

"That's what I'm trying to figure out. You went to the party over there the other night, didn't you?"

"Yes."

"Did you go with Frank?"

"Several of us went together. Ben Kantor, Nick Farr, along with a couple of others. And Frank."

"How did he seem to you?"

"Drunk. In fact, I was annoyed with him."

"Why was that?"

"He was playing the role. It began to get on my nerves."

"Did you tell him?"

"Yes, we had a fight about it on the way over. I didn't hang around after that."

"Did you see him?"

"Sure, but at a distance. I avoided him."

"Had you had fights like this before?"

"Just work-related stuff. If I thought he was going in the

120

wrong direction with the book, I told him."

"How did he handle that?"

"It depended. Some of it we came to an agreement on. Other things we didn't."

"Did you see him with anyone in particular at the party?"

"You mean like Asia?"

I nodded.

"No, I didn't. But I heard that she was there."

"How familiar are you with the house?"

"Reasonably. I've been through it a few times. Wallace always enjoys showing me around."

"What about the buildings in back?"

Jocelyn fixed me with another of her stares. "You mean Hemingway's writing studio? Yes, Wallace showed me everything."

"What time did you leave that night?"

Jocelyn regarded me with that cold stare once again. "Am I a suspect?"

"According to the police, everyone who was at the party is a suspect."

"I left about ten-thirty. And I didn't kill Frank."

"Where did you go?"

"I came back here."

"Alone?"

"That's none of your business."

I stood up and studied the harbor, the sailboats at anchor, the whine of another powerboat pounding across the wake of a passing charter boat. "Someone said you were on your way to Mexico."

"At the end of the week when the festival is over."

"Good, I may want to talk to you before then."

Jocelyn didn't get up. "By all means. It's been such a pleasure. I wouldn't want to miss another opportunity."

31.

Returning home, I wondered about Jocelyn Beatty. She had obviously been around the block a time or two. Inside that cool exterior was a tough, manipulative woman. I wondered, too, about the marriage to the Hemingway grandson. I decided to call Nick Farr and ask him about it. As well as about Jocelyn's relationship to Frank Maguire.

On my way home I tried to play a few possible scenes over in my head, but they didn't play well. George Lewis was in too big a hurry to close this case. I was pretty sure I knew why. It had all the ingredients for a sensational murder that would stay on the front pages for weeks. Hemingway. A beautiful starlet, oil, and the literary fringe society of Key West. It could not only disrupt business at the Hemingway House, but it would keep George Lewis on the hot seat for weeks if he didn't solve it fast. That was not where a man like George wanted to be at this stage in his career, which was no doubt why Sweetwater had been brought in so fast in the manner of old-style Southern justice.

A lot of people might not have been unhappy to see Frank Maguire dead—Asia, Mickey Freeman, even Jocelyn came to mind, people who could actually be ascribed a motive, however tenuous, for killing him—while Sweetwater was left dangling from the end of a rope.

As I was approaching my office, I saw a man walk up on the front porch and ring the doorbell. He had on jeans and a white Western shirt with pearl snap buttons. He turned as I was locking my bike. Light glinted off a wide silver buckle on his belt, which was studded with turquoise and seemed to pinch the overhanging lap of his paunch. Mickey Freeman. I stared at the sleek, supple boots made from some exotic animal skin.

"You Gideon Lowry, pardner?"

I nodded. He offered his hand, and we shook. His was large, the flesh swollen where rings adorned the fingers of both his hands. When he grinned, his teeth seemed unnaturally white. "It's good to meet you, pardner."

I opened the door and went in ahead of him. He sat down, dwarfing the wicker chair in front of my desk. He wore a freeze-dried smile. "I heard you've been asking about me."

"Your name's come up a couple of times in connection with Frank Maguire."

"Poor Frank. It couldn't have happened to a nicer guy." The smile remained. "And somehow fitting. Death in the afternoon at the Hemingway House."

"It happened at night."

Mickey Freeman shrugged his massive shoulders. "A fine distinction. You any relation to Carl Lowry?"

I said I was his brother.

"Carl was a good man. I understand he had a change of views toward the end of his life, but I can't imagine we wouldn't have been able to work together."

I didn't reply.

"Carl was a good ally while it lasted."

"For the oil industry?"

"Don't make it sound so evil, pardner. Where would this country be without oil? Look ninety miles to the south of you, what's happened to Cuba, and be thankful we've got that slimy stuff coming out of the ground here."

"I guess the message you got yesterday was keep it coming out of the ground, not offshore."

"Misconceptions. Some of those rigs have been pumping for years without incident."

"Yes, and then there was Valdez—"

"Right. It ruined us. The worst possible PR."

"Frank Maguire didn't exactly help your cause."

"You read his stuff? I admit Frank was a pain in the ass over the years, but who remembers anything they read in the newspapers. Not like TV."

"You didn't take it personally then?"

"Meaning?"

"There's a rumor you were buying the Hemingway House. Maguire was going to live there. You'd found a way to get him off your back."

The smile didn't move. "Well, now, those are just rumors. My friend Ruth Clampitt who owns the place might have something to say about that."

"Maybe not if she's having financial problems."

"Now where do you hear that?"

I shrugged. "It wouldn't be the first time you tried to buy your way out of problems. I hear that, too."

"Well, tell me everything."

"Asia. She got her first start because of you is what I hear."

"Hey, because I'm a businessman, I'm not supposed to recognize talent? Give me a break. You do get around, though, don't you, pardner?"

"The name's Gideon," I said, tiring of the folksy Texas tag line. "And in case you hadn't heard, there's a murder investigation under way here."

"What's that got to do with me?"

"You flew into town on a private plane the day Frank was killed, didn't you?"

"The day before. So what?"

"Frank's wife flew out on the same plane about twenty-four hours after the murder. A little too much of a coincidence, isn't it? You just happen to share a lease on the same plane?"

Mickey lifted his big hands. "No crime in that, is there?"

I shook my head. There wasn't any crime, it was all perfectly natural. And I didn't believe it. "Were you at the Hemingway party?"

"Yeah, I was there along with a lot of other people."

"Did you talk to Frank?"

"Sure, I talked to him. I've known him a long time. Why wouldn't I talk to him?"

"What did you talk about?"

"The same thing we always talk about. Him."

"And?"

"And what? He was drunk. Playing his favorite role. Papa."

"What about Asia, did you see her, too?"

"I talked to her. Frank got pissed off and tried to start a fight. I left."

"What time would that have been?"

"Ten o'clock, ten-thirty. I don't remember."

"How long are you in town?"

"As long as business takes me." Mickey stood up. "Is that okay with you?"

"For the moment."

Mickey Freeman's smile never wavered as he sauntered out the door. I picked up the phone and called Nick Farr.

32.

I arrived early at the Cuban joint downtown where Nick and I had agreed to meet for lunch and staked out an empty booth in the back. There was a steady hiss from the steamer on the five-cup espresso machine in constant use. The walls were decorated with bullfight posters. A waitress, taking a pencil from the dark hair stacked high on her head, came over and I ordered a *café con leche*.

She returned with the coffee just as Nick was coming in the door. I waved and watched him walk back toward me. The jeans he wore seemed a little scruffier than usual, riding low on his hips, the cuffs turned up as though he'd just waded ashore. With his tousled hair, grimy T-shirt, and face puffy from drink or lack of sleep—or both—he looked more like a shrimper who had just returned from two weeks at sea than part of the literary establishment. He sat down and asked the waitress for a Corona.

"Unbelievable," Nick said.

"Maguire?"

Nick nodded. "What have you heard?"

"They're holding Sweetwater."

"No! The fight ref? They think he killed Frank?"

"The chief of detectives is more interested in closing the case than answering those kinds of questions. Too much bad publicity."

"Are you getting involved?"

"Sweetwater's a friend of mine. I've known him all my life."

When the waitress returned with Nick's Corona, we ordered. Rice, beans, plantains, and a side dish of yuca, a vegetable common to tropical climates that was marinated in garlic and lime juice.

"Any leads?" Nick asked when the waitress left.

"Bundles of them, but they all somehow fizzle out at that party the other night. Frank apparently was a mess, belligerent and disagreeable. Is that a fair assessment? You were there."

"Well, I didn't spend a lot of time with him, but he was definitely a dominant presence."

"Asia was there. She argued with him. So did Jocelyn. Then there's a guy by the name of Mickey Freeman, an oil executive who Frank knew. They fought. In their own way I suppose each of them is better off now that he's dead."

"Jocelyn?"

"Apparently she wasn't all that pleased with the direction Frank was taking on the Hemingway novel."

"I didn't know that. But even so, all she had to do was take him off the project. Killing him does seem rather extreme."

"Maybe." The waitress brought our food. "What do you know about that manuscript?" I asked when she left.

"Nothing. Why?"

"Could it be a fake?"

Nick laughed. "Sure, it could be. As far as I know, the only people to have seen it are Jos and Frank. And the Hemingway family, presumably."

"If it was legitimate, do you think they'd let something like that out of their possession? Even in a divorce settlement?"

Nick laughed again. "Sounds like you don't exactly trust Jos."

"She's a tough nut."

"Complex."

"What was her personal relationship with Frank?"

Nick took a long swallow of beer. "I don't know that it was personal. She seemed less than happy with him the other night."

"What about her husband? Did you know him?"

Nick shook his head.

"Could you find out about him?"

"I'll see what I can do." Nick grinned. "What about the others who were involved with Frank?"

"The oil exec, a guy by the name of Mickey Freeman, showed up here on a private plane the day before Frank was killed. Asia left on that same plane shortly after Frank was killed."

"Coincidence?"

"Mickey had helped launch Asia a few years ago when she and Frank were still together."

"The plot sickens. Do the cops know about Freeman?"

"He's got connections in Tallahassee and Washington. They might know about him, but I don't think a small-town cop is going to pose a problem for Mickey Freeman."

"Where does that leave you?"

"With a few hundred people who were at that party the other night. Someone must have seen something. What about you? Did you see Frank?"

"Briefly, after the fights. I was talking to the ref when Frank came over."

"You talked to Sweetwater? What about?"

"The usual. His association with Hemingway." The waitress put a fresh beer in front of Nick.

"Jesus, what is it with you guys? You can't walk past the dead in your profession without touching their bones."

Nick smiled sadly. "True. Hemingway is like a talisman. Every other writer wants to emulate him. Or topple him from the throne."

"Why?"

"A measure of success, I suppose. You remember what Andy Warhol said. He was right. Everybody gets their fifteen minutes of fame now. Everybody's a star means nobody's a star. It also means it gets tougher and tougher to make a living."

"What did you and Frank talk about?"

Nick shrugged and drained his beer. "Frank was blowing his own horn all night. I tried to steer clear of him."

The waitress came by and took away our plates.

"Did you see any of the sparring between Frank and Sweetwater?"

"No, I missed that."

"What time did you leave?"

"Around eleven, I think."

"Was anyone else around then?"

"A few hangers-on. Not many. The staff was busy trying to get the place closed up."

"Did Jocelyn tell you she's thinking of getting you to finish the Hemingway book?"

"No. She told you that?"

"She mentioned it as a possibility. How's your own work going?"

"Slowly. I'm on the roof and the creek's rising."

"Deadlines?"

He nodded.

"You'll beat it," I said.

"I have to. Or else I'm finished."

"Any more messages from your anonymous friend?"

"Funny you should ask." Nick reached into his shirt pocket. He brought out a folded sheet of paper and handed it to me.

I opened it. The same even printing as the one Nick showed me the other day: *Bang, bang. You're next.*

"When did you get this?"

"Yesterday."

"Have you been to the police?"

"No."

"I advise you to go. In case it's connected with Maguire's murder."

Nick nodded. Something troubling was in his expression,

something quizzical, as though he had a question but couldn't ask it. I saw something manipulative in his grim boyish face, his eyes staring at me as if I held the answer to all his unspoken questions. I had, of course, seen a similar expression before, in the face of my brother, Carl—a man unequaled in his ability to manipulate.

33.

Nick's ex-wife's home was on William Street, a block from where I'd grown up. I rode down the street of my youth, the street that beckoned me on the journey back to my beginnings. On impulse I stopped at Maggie's. She came to the door of the small two-story frame house, her red hair in a mass of angry tangles, her narrow face set in a frown. From somewhere beyond her, the voice of a child cried out in what sounded like frustration.

Maggie had on shorts, a painted T-shirt, and no shoes. It had been several months since I'd seen her, and I had forgotten just how attractive she could be in her domestic role.

"Gideon. I haven't seen you in ages. What brings you around? Did you ever reach Nick?"

"I just had lunch with him. I was on my way home and thought I'd stop. Is it inconvenient?"

Maggie looked back inside the house where everything was quiet. "No. Come in." She pushed open the screen door and I stepped inside.

The small living room looked more like a playpen, the floor littered with toys. A variety of stuffed animals sat like sentinels on the steps leading up to the second floor. I followed Maggie into the kitchen where a child sat in the middle of the floor constructing something out of plastic pieces that snapped together. He glanced up at me briefly with tears in his eyes when I came in, before his concentration returned to his play.

"Some coffee, Gideon?"

"If it's no trouble."

131

Maggie took a couple of cups from the dish drainer in the sink. "Go sit out on the deck. I'll bring it out. Cream or sugar?"

"Sugar." I went out the back door onto a small deck where there was a plastic table beneath a beach umbrella and two chairs.

"Are you here about Nick?" Maggie asked, handing me the cup.

"He seems in bad shape. I'm worried about him."

Maggie sat down in the other chair and stared out across the backyard, which was mostly a jungle of tropical shrubs with a wild tangle of vines growing along the back fence and up the drain spout of the house. The house needed paint. I noticed that some of the boards beneath the windowsills and the transom were showing signs of rot.

"I've quit worrying about him," Maggie said. "I've had to. I've got enough just to worry about me and Justin."

"He seems to be under a lot of pressure."

Maggie shrugged. "He's always under pressure. You have no idea what it was like living with him. He was so"—one of her hands came up and clutched at the air—"intense," she gasped. "It was frightening sometimes."

"His work?"

"He was married to his damned work." She closed her eyes. "If I ever get married again, it will be to someone who goes out at nine, comes home at five, and leaves the work at the office."

"You thinking of doing that?" I drank some coffee. It was hot. I felt the sweat start out along my forehead. Maggie leaned her face on one palm and began to twist a ringlet of hair with the fingers of her other hand. "Getting married. I've thought of it, but I've got no particular candidate in mind. Besides, Nick might balk at a divorce."

"Why?"

"Because he still likes to feel in control of our lives in some way. He would get used to it, I suppose, but I don't think he could handle being replaced right now."

"Doesn't that make any kind of a life hard for you?"

Maggie looked wistful. "Yes, and I'm thinking of leaving."

"Leaving Key West? Where would you go?"

"Oh, probably back to Vermont. That's where I'm from."

"Have you told Nick?"

One tear started to slide down Maggie's cheek before she quickly wiped it away. "Yes. He knows. I don't think he's particularly happy about it. But this is a nowhere life for me."

We sat for a moment sipping our coffee while Maggie, eyes downcast, took several deep breaths. When she looked up at me, she said, "Life's just so fucking hard sometimes. You think you've got it all figured out and then, boom!" Her mouth twisted as she fought to hold back the tears.

"I probably shouldn't have come."

Maggie tried to smile. "Oh, Gideon, it's all right. I'm glad you came by. It's just that all anyone wants to talk about is Nick. There's a struggle going on here, too, even though it may not be as interesting as the one Nick is going through."

"Do you want to talk about it?"

"Just the usual domestic routine. The kind of thing that doesn't interest Nick."

"He's a good father, isn't he?"

"As long as it's on his terms." Maggie turned toward me, her face darkening. "Nick didn't ask you to come over here, did he, Gideon?"

"If he had, I would have told you. I didn't even tell him I was coming. I just thought I should talk to you."

"It's all right. I appreciate it, Gideon. I'm just sorry I sound so bitter."

I watched as she raised her clenched fist to her upper lip. "Do you think there's any possibility of a reconciliation?"

A startled expression crossed her eyes for a moment when she looked at me, then she laughed. "Did you ask Nick that question?"

"No. I didn't. It just occurred to me."

"Then you should."

"I will. But right now I'm asking you."

There was a long pause. Finally, she said, "I don't know. At this point I really don't know. And as for Nick, the problem is his damned pride. He won't admit a mistake, much less defeat."

Another silence descended over us until a plane banked overhead on its approach to the airport. I finished my coffee. "You're managing," I said, thinking I'd intruded enough.

"With the typing work I can take in at home, and the child support, I can get by. As you can see, that's about all. Without Nick's help, we're on welfare. And that isn't right. I've got to have a life of my own."

"Nick's working on a couple of different books. He's trying to meet deadlines."

"Oh, he's been meeting deadlines forever. It's always the next project that's going to save him."

"Maybe it will."

"Nick lives on hope and maybe. It isn't enough for me and Justin. I need something more concrete."

"Did you hear about the murder at the Hemingway House the other night?" I asked, trying to change the subject.

"How could I not? It's all anyone is talking about. I suppose Nick was there."

"Yes, he knew the guy who was killed."

Maggie sighed. "There's something almost adolescent about this homage to Hemingway, don't you think? I mean look-a-like contests, boxing matches—" She shook her head. "And now the death of a writer in the same kind of way. It's all just so—so competitive."

The child came out on the deck and said, "Mommy, can I have some juice?" The boy was about five years old, with missing teeth, a scattershot of freckles across his pug nose, and a thick head of uncombed reddish blond hair. He wore overalls and a rather somber expression, a younger version of Nick's, I thought.

Maggie got up and went inside. "More coffee, Gideon?" she called.

"No, I have to go."

Maggie came back wiping her hands on a cloth. "Don't pay any attention to me. It's just that sometimes all this boy stuff gets to me. Please don't say anything to Nick."

"Of course not." I stood up. "Those notes and phone calls you were receiving a while back. They stopped, didn't they?"

"The calls, yes." She seemed to hesitate. "Why?"

"Nick has gotten some more notes. Did he tell you?"

Maggie nodded. "Yes, it's all very distressing. Has he asked you to look into it again?"

"No. I think he believes it will blow over, the way it did the last time."

Maggie sighed. "I wish there was something I could do."

"You still love him?"

"I don't know."

We walked back inside. Justin, his eyes downcast, was having a conversation with an imaginary friend.

"The world of make-believe." Maggie smiled. "Sometimes I find myself doing the same thing. Having conversations with ghosts, trying to make everything the way I would like it."

I nodded, knowing what it was like to be haunted by ghosts.

34.

Dappled afternoon light filtered through ancient shade trees and played over the fretwork of the concrete building on the corner of Simonton and Angela streets that housed the city police and one of Key West's fire stations. I walked in past the double glass doors and up the stairs to the office of Capt. George Lewis.

The door was locked and no one responded to my knock. Office staff moved through the corridors. I stopped a secretary, who told me she thought George was in the chief's office downstairs. I walked back down the worn marble steps and checked with the police dispatcher behind her Plexiglas shield. She shouted to someone through a doorway behind her before turning back to tell me that, yeah, George was with the chief.

I decided to hang around. Lewis would have to come into the hallway, so I bought a soda from a dispensing machine and waited. I'd finished half of it when he came out, smiling as though he'd just heard a good joke. The smile quickly disappeared when he saw me. He held up his hands as if to ward me off.

"I'm not talking to you," he said. "I don't have time."

"There's a couple of things you should know."

"Probably more than a couple." George started up the stairs. I followed.

"Give me a minute. Just one minute and I won't push this again."

George looked at his watch. We stopped outside the door to his office. George took out a handkerchief and blew his nose.

"Talk. You're on the watch."

"Mickey Freeman."

"Who's Mickey Freeman?"

I told him what I knew. "How much time do I have left?"

"Fifteen seconds." George opened the door to his office.

I told him about the discrepancy between the Hemingway House staff's accounts and what Sweetwater had said, about the lights being on the night of the murder and Wallace still at the house when Sweets left. And about the storage room where the shotgun was kept. George cut me off.

"We know about that."

"There were two hundred people at that party the other night. Maguire was behaving like a pompous ass. There might have been a few of them who would not have been unhappy to see Maguire dead. It seems like enough to warrant an investigation—"

"Your time's up, Bud. We are investigating and you're hampering that investigation. I've been getting reports that you're making a nuisance of yourself. You don't have any official status, so back off."

"You've known Sweetwater as long as I have. Which is all your damn life."

"Bud, cool down."

"You know as well as I do that Sweetwater didn't kill Maguire. He couldn't kill anyone."

"I'm a cop, like you once were. I ain't paid to know who can do what, but to investigate and act on the facts. You know that."

"What facts?"

"The fight Maguire was in before he was shot."

"So what? You can't accuse Sweetwater of murder simply because he and Maguire were boxing."

"Sweetwater had access to the storage room where the gun was kept. It's enough evidence to bring him in for questioning and that's what we've done."

"I think this is bullshit. Did you find prints on the gun?"

People were standing around now, on the fringe of the dispute, and my anger.

"Bud, we're doing our job here. We don't need any trouble from you. I've already warned you. Stay out of the way on this one."

"Just tell me one thing. What reason would Sweetwater have for killing Frank Maguire?"

George shook his head. "Look, you got your lawyer on the case. Unless we come up with something substantial, Sweetwater will be out later today. So what are you so all-fired het up about?" George turned, went inside his office, and slammed the door.

I wondered what my father would have done if he were alive. Taken a swing at George Lewis? Probably. Not because of Sweetwater, but because George had slammed a door in his face. Sweetwater wasn't his people, as Captain Billy liked to say; George was. You stuck with your people even if you had to deck them once in a while to keep them in line.

Phyllis would not have wasted a minute on George Lewis's loutish behavior. She would have gone behind the scenes, deftly trying to get Sweetwater released. Phyllis had a way of getting things done, in contrast to Captain Billy, whose physical nature was simply his way of stage-managing events outside his immediate control.

It was strange, I thought, to have arrived at such a familiarity with my family now that they were all dead, having known them so little when they were alive. Part of me longed to confront George, to pound some sense into him, all the while being aware of the unlikelihood that such a course of action would bring success.

Instead, I walked out of the building and stood beneath the twisted and brittle branches of the poinciana tree, feeling a quiet rage. A rage that was directed at myself as much as it was at George Lewis. Rage that was the product of guilt for not having been able to prevent the death of my brother, and perhaps even my father. That was what I was het up about, in George's words. And of course Sweetwater was an extension of all that.

I raked my hand across the bark of the poinciana tree. Barking up the wrong tree. I went home and settled down at my desk to read the notebooks I'd gotten from Ben Kantor. Frank Maguire's last words, not counting the Hemingway novel.

35.

Beginning with Hemingway's arrival in Key West on a ferry from Havana, Frank's notes detailed the locales and people the writer had encountered here on his way to putting Key West on the literary road map.

Many of the same places and people were around when I was growing up. Some of their families were still here. Reading about them brought back a familiar nostalgia. And as he had in that first book, Maguire also seemed to weave in his own interpretation of what Hemingway might have been thinking, of people he might have had dealings with, a kind of blending of fact and fiction, but until I was halfway through the book, I didn't see the relevance to the present that Ben had alluded to, until I began to skim over the chapters.

Then it hit me what Maguire was really up to. He was writing history, and rewriting history; not only according to his own vision, but to the way it might have been. He was asking the question: What if? And then providing an answer. Sometimes several answers. As I read, it became clear that Maguire, in providing a series of scenarios for the various episodes in a life that had previously been examined in detail, had found a way of writing himself into history as well.

Maguire not only diverged from the common perception of Hemingway's life in Key West in the thirties, he was extending that life right into the present by drawing parallels with his—Frank's—own life. By the time I was halfway I was reading about Maguire and Asia, and Hemingway and Marlene Dietrich, almost as though they were interchangeable characters in a Frank Maguire novel. The writer and the diva. Flowing back and forth in time. I saw Asia again as she was the night she sang at the club. The voice could have been Dietrich's. I was mesmerized.

There was the writer as journalist and the writer as novelist—reflections in a mirror. Characters dovetailing with their creator. Maguire was bending time and space to serve up a stew in which he'd blended the ingredients from two different eras and only he had known how it would come out.

Of course I knew what had happened to Hemingway. And to Frank Maguire. Or did I? Maguire seemed to be calling into question the whole notion of perceived reality. I was reminded of the times I'd looked over my own shoulder at the receding past, only hours ago, wondering how I might have manipulated the events in my own life to have brought about a different outcome.

Maguire had perceived his own death. But had he also perceived it in its myriad possibilities with a variety of suspects? Could he have written a scenario for each of them: Mickey Freeman? Asia? Even Jocelyn?

And perhaps there were others I hadn't considered. I turned the pages seeking answers, but Maguire had moved on to Cuba.

Cuba. In the fifties, Captain Billy had made the ninety-mile crossing from Key West on the *Low Blow* more than once before he died. He had gone there to fish, and after my return from Korea he took me along on one of those trips. I remember, as we approached, the way the ancient city of Havana rose up out of the sea like a mirage, with its mountains to the east, such an incredible geological mass so close to the Keys where nothing more than the span of a bridge broke the monotony of the flat landscape between Key West and Miami.

Skimming through Frank Maguire's notes, I found that he had described similar feelings about the view off the coast of Cuba, a view that had remained relatively unchanged from the one Hemingway would have seen. Maguire made much of that, not just the view, but the points of view as he explored the Hemingway landmarks in Cuba beginning with the Ambos Mundos Hotel where he stayed in Hemingway's room, and La Bodeguita del Medio and the Floridita where he had drinks.

He prowled around the Finca Vigia, Hemingway's farmhouse outside Havana in San Francisco de Paula, comparing it with the house in Key West. The Finca, in Maguire's view, was superior, looking out over Havana as it did and down to the fishing village where Hemingway kept his boat and where his guide Gregorio Fuentes lived. Maguire talked to Fuentes, still living in Cojimar.

More than thirty years had passed since Hemingway had left Cuba soon after the revolution, but Maguire seemed to have no trouble gaining access to anything he wanted for his research.

Weaving between past and present, the real and the imagined, Maguire also sketched a brief history of Cuba from Hemingway's days there to Maguire's own arrival, which had taken place in the last several months. Maguire had gone there, via Mexico, with an American businessman who was looking into the possibility of offshore oil drilling along Cuba's coast.

Maguire identified the businessman as Mickey Freeman. Mickey had smoothed the way for Frank, and Frank, by putting this in writing, may have been in the process of betraying Freeman.

It certainly provided a strong motive for murder, but it left me no closer to proving that Mickey Freeman was implicated in Frank's death; and therefore no closer to clearing Sweetwater than I had been earlier.

I wondered if Mickey was aware of the existence of these pages. As I sat mulling it over, the phone rang. Casey's voice purred gently on the other end of the line. I apologized for not getting back to her, telling her a little of what I was working on.

"Bud," she said when I was finished, "are you all right?" Casey knew of my history with Sweetwater, the distant but nonetheless real emotional tie he'd had with my family.

"I'm fine."

"I'm coming down."

I hesitated. "With the new boyfriend?"

"Yes. But I would like to see you."

"I'm always glad to see you."

"Good, we can have coffee together." I thought I could detect a smile in Casey's voice. "I'll see you in a couple of days," she said.

36.

The Pier House was crowded that night, but they had not come to hear me play. Ronnie was working the blender overtime concocting the special drinks celebrating Hemingway: Papa Dobles. By the sound of it they were a success. I finished up the set with "Cry Me a River," then managed to get a club soda from Ronnie before scooting outside to stare into the harbor and escape some of the din for a few minutes.

I was standing there when someone spoke my name. I turned. The guy standing beside me was middle-aged, passing for young. Dark hair was pulled back in a ponytail dangling to his shoulders. A bushy mustache stretched across his upper lip like the long horns on a bull. He wore jeans and a tie-dyed T-shirt that did nothing to hide the roll of flesh creeping over his waistband.

"Dan Riggs, with *Rolling Stone*." He stuck out his hand and we shook. The onslaught had begun. "I got into town this evening and was told I could find you here. Can we talk?"

Riggs carried a reporter's notebook, which he tapped against the railing. "I'm told the police have someone in custody."

"The wrong someone."

"How do you know?"

"I know the man they're holding."

Riggs nodded, his ponytail bobbing. "You have any other leads?"

"A few. None that I want to reveal to the press."

"What about Mickey Freeman?"

144

"What about him?"

"Do you know where he is?"

"He's in Key West. Staying at the Casa Marina Hotel."

Riggs didn't show any surprise. "Have you talked to him?"

"Once."

"And?"

"Look, I don't know why you're down here, what you expect to accomplish—"

"I'm reporting a story, the death of a colleague."

"Well, I'm sorry about Frank Maguire. Maybe he was a good man, I don't know. I only met him once, I didn't know him. But I have known the guy the police are holding all my life, and I'll do what I have to do to get him out of this. I don't see how talking to you is going to help that effort."

Dan nodded. "I understand. I'll be in town for a while. From time to time I may check in with you. Just in case."

"Fine. But I'm not making any promises."

Dan Riggs touched his notebook to his forehead in a mock salute. "Don't worry, no one else is either."

Maybe I'd been too hard on him, I thought as I returned to the piano. I'd grown frustrated in my efforts to clear Sweetwater. I hoped Riggs hadn't taken it personally when it was probably just my mood. The bar was getting increasingly noisier as the Papa Dobles worked their magic, and in the din the piano was barely audible. At one o'clock I stopped competing and called it a night.

I biked home, keeping to the more well-lighted Duval Street, without incident. I chained my bike to the front porch and let myself in the front door. Something was wrong. I sensed it as soon as I opened the door. Some strange, lingering odor that was not a part of my environment.

As I pushed the door closed with my foot and reached for the light switch, there was a sudden whoosh of air before something slammed against the back of my head, and the sky fell in.

Night and Day

I was cast loose, adrift in the sea, with only the scattered phosphorescent glow of plankton darting around my hands as I tried to keep myself afloat. I heard my mother's voice: "Oil and water don't mix!" And saw Captain Billy, grisly white, in the wheelhouse of a ghostship making slow progress through thick, oil-besmirched seas and a gray fog. Carl was beside him, grinning. I struggled to get their attention, but each time I tried to call I was overcome by the blackened waves, drowning in a sea of oil. With one final effort I pushed myself forward, swimming for the ship Captain Billy piloted to nowhere, Carl's maniacal laughter ringing in my ears, his voice echoing, "Don't be late, Bud. Don't be late," as the ghostship drifted out of sight.

The second hand on my watch moved around in a hazy circle, a fluorescent glow, the darting plankton I thought I'd seen as I came to, lying in a pool of my own vomit. I managed to get on my knees, steady myself as I tried to clear my head from the pain that shot through it like an electric shock. I couldn't have been out more than ten minutes judging from the time on my watch. It was one-twenty. Later than you think.

I got to the bathroom and cleaned myself up, then staggered back to my office and turned on a light. A short piece of hardwood flooring that I was going to use to make some repairs lay on the floor near the front door. I cleaned up the mess on the floor, looked around, saw that the back door had been forced open, but other than that nothing seemed amiss.

I thought about calling the cops, then thought better of it while standing by the phone on my desk. My empty desk, the desk where Frank Maguire's notebooks had been.

37.

In the morning I was feeling my age. Pushed off a bicycle and mugged by a young crack addict only days ago and last night blindsided in my own home. Every joint in my body ached, and my head felt as if it had been pressed in a vise for several hours. I had lost my touch. I was too old for this, maybe it was time to hang it up, draw back inside myself and live out my days on the fringe of life. Social security was just around the corner. Then I remembered Sweetwater.

The phone was ringing. I staggered up and limped into the office.

It was Will Clark. "They released him last night."

"Any charges?"

"None."

So George Lewis had finally come to his senses. I pressed a hand to the lump on the back of my head. Now I could retire. I thanked Will Clark and told him to send me a bill for his services, then I got dressed and went to the drugstore where I suspected Sweetwater would stop even though it was after nine o'clock, beyond both our normal breakfast hours.

Sweetwater sat at the counter eating grits and eggs. He grinned when I sat down beside him. "I'm a free man, Bud."

"So you are, Sweets. So you are. I'm glad to see it."

"Much appreciate your help. I can do anything for you, you let me know."

"You can."

"What's that, Bud?"

"Talk to me about that night just one more time."

147

Sweets sighed. "What you want to know, Bud? I thought we'd been over everything."

"I want to know about Maguire. Just how drunk was he?"

"What do you mean?"

"Everyone who came in contact with him that night said he was belligerent, that they avoided him. Was he that way with you?"

"No, sir. He'd been drinking, I know that much, but I would never have got in the ring with him if he'd been drunk."

"Did you think he was playing a role?"

"You mean like he was Papa? Yeah, there was some of that in him."

"Where did you talk?"

"Where? Different places. By the ring. In the changing room."

"In the changing room?"

"Yeah, he want to see the place. I showed him in there."

"Did you show him the storage room?"

"He looked in there."

"Did he go inside, spend any time in there?"

"Yeah, he wandered in. I didn't pay much attention. He asking me questions all the time."

"Do you know if he picked up the gun?"

Sweets shook his head. "Didn't see him."

"Did you tell George Lewis about this?"

"Didn't ask. I only answer the questions he ask."

"There must have been other people around, Sweets. Are you sure you didn't see anyone with Maguire?"

"Plenty of people around all night. They talk to me. I even talk to another writer."

"Nick Farr?"

"Yeah, that his name. But like I told you, by the time Maguire came around, most everyone was gone."

"Did you see anyone in the main house?"

"No."

"The light was on. Someone was in there late when you left."

"Wallace, I suppose."

"He said he never went in there."

Sweetwater shrugged. "Can't help you there, Bud."

Maybe no one could. So why was I bothering? This was a police matter now. Let George Lewis handle it. I had no more stake in it. Except for a crack on the head and some missing papers that had been left in my care. I drank some coffee, still feeling slightly nauseated.

"I'd like to see you get your job back there," I told Sweets before I left. "That is, if you want it."

Sweetwater nodded. "Hard to pass up that kind of money."

When I got back to the house, the mail had come. Only one item caught my attention, a letter from the brokerage firm where I'd been the other day. I sat at my desk and tore open the envelope. It was the information I'd requested on Globe Oil, a breakdown showing the extent of Globe's diversification.

There was a heavy concentration of subsidiary companies in the Orlando area, clearly satellites of the Disney enterprise. Some fast-food chains, and a couple of airplanes for corporate lease. Also, on Florida's west coast in the Tampa and St. Petersburg area, they held a major investment in the franchise of a fast-growing video-rental business. And in Miami another sizable investment in a cable-television company. Most of their assets were in coastal regions where tourism was important: Georgia, the Carolinas, and Louisiana. And of course California. From the figures in the spreadsheets it was clear that Globe, apart from the inactive leases and some wells off the coast of Louisiana, had turned more to entertainment than the oil business. However, nothing really caught my eye except for one of the companies in California. MTV.

From what I could understand, Globe had apparently invested heavily in the early days of the company, several years ago. About the time, I remembered, that Asia was getting started.

I thought it was time to pay a call on Mickey Freeman and begin turning some screws. Maybe I'd been a little too easy on him the last time we talked.

I rode over to the Casa. Rob, the guy who liked taking money from me, wasn't on the door when I went in. I used the house phone and asked for Mickey Freeman's room, then listened to the phone in his room ring five empty times before I hung up. I wandered around the pool and beach area and into the bar and restaurant without seeing the cowboy. The fact that it was after noon reassured me that he hadn't checked out.

I got on my bike and rode across town to the Hemingway House.

38.

It was business as usual with Wallace collecting the gate receipts once again. "When did you reopen?" I asked once there was a break in the stream of tourists.

"This morning," Wallace said. "And haven't you caused enough trouble around here?"

"Not nearly enough. Is Ruth in?"

"Do you have an appointment?"

"I will have." I moved past him. Wallace seemed about to try to stop me, then waved his hand in dismissal. I walked up to Ruth's office, where she and Liz were conferring. "Afternoon, ladies."

Liz turned, smiling. Ruth looked at me without expression.

"Sorry to barge in, but I've got a request now that you're back in business. My friend Sweetwater is out of jail and would like his job back."

"Mr. Lowry, you have a lot of chutzpah," Ruth said.

"I'm sorry. I didn't know it showed. I just got these pants back from the laundry the other day. I thought they felt a little tight."

Liz snickered. "It isn't funny," Ruth reproached her. And to me: "Under the circumstances, I don't see how we could do that."

"Why not? Sweets wasn't accused of any crime. He hasn't done anything. And you had an agreement with him to referee the fights here."

"That was before the incident."

"It would attract a lot of people," Liz said encouragingly.

"We're trying to put this behind us," Ruth said. "Murder isn't something we want to promote."

"The fact remains it was an unsolved murder," I said. "There's still an investigation under way. Did you ever find out who was in the house that night if it wasn't Wallace?"

"No," Ruth said. "And I've been advised by Captain Lewis that you have no authority to ask questions about the case."

I shrugged. "How about Mickey Freeman? Is your deal with him still going through?"

Ruth glared at me. "You've made it very awkward for me over that issue."

"How's that?"

"By leaking the news that this house is for sale."

"I didn't leak it, Wallace did."

"I've spoken to Wallace about it."

"Which explains the chilly reception I got coming in. Anyway, it's true, isn't it?"

"Is there anything else?"

"Oh, plenty, but it doesn't seem to be getting me anywhere." I turned to go. "I'd appreciate it if you'd reconsider about Sweetwater."

Ruth had turned away and was reaching for the phone. Liz followed me outside. I stopped beside the pool house. "Why do I get the feeling I'm going to have to begin paying if I want to get in here again?" I asked Liz.

Liz laughed. "Don't worry about it. Everyone's on a short fuse right now."

I wasn't sure how far I could trust Liz. With her effusive, happy-go-lucky attitude, she seemed either incredibly simple or disingenuous; perhaps both. But I needed someone on the inside whom I could trust; simplicity could sometimes make a good ally. "What do you know about Ruth?" I asked.

The smile never left Liz's face. "Oh, her bark's worse than her bite. Don't let her get to you."

"I was wondering more about her background."

"Ruth was the director for a couple of historical homes before she came here."

"Where was that?"

"On the west coast." Liz seemed to divide her attention between me and the crowds who prowled the grounds. Always with the ready smile. Her affability was not phony, I thought, but it was more than disarming.

"California?"

"No, Florida. She had some connection with Edison's place near Sarasota. And someplace else, I've forgotten now."

"Do those jobs pay the kind of money it would take to buy a place like this?"

Liz shook her head. "I really don't know about the financial details."

I scratched my head. "Strange, but Ruth told me that you really ran things here."

Liz scoffed. "Oh, I keep the day-to-day stuff going, but Ruth is the brains behind it. She knows how to promote it. This use of the house for several of the Hemingway Days events was her idea."

"The boxing matches?"

Liz nodded. "That kind of thing, yes."

"Wallace said she wasn't much of a manager. The place was in difficulty financially."

"I told you not to pay any attention to Wallace. He can be a bit of a troublemaker."

"It isn't true then."

"What?"

"The rumor that the place is for sale."

Liz showed me more of her pretty white teeth. "You've lived here all your life. Do you know any place that isn't for sale? At the right price, of course."

"And Mickey Freeman?"

"What about him?"

"Would he be an interested buyer?"

153

"I think you should ask him," Liz said, looking at her watch. "I've really got to run."

"Of course. I'm sorry to take so much of your time."

"Not at all." Liz beamed and shook my hand. "Anytime."

I glanced at the pool house, listening to the muted hum of the pumps inside, then turned and walked to the front. Wallace stared at me as if I had leprosy as I went out the gate. Except for Liz, a real friendly place.

I made my way through the crowds and the heat down to Sloppy Joe's bar at the other end of town where Nick Farr and Jocelyn Beatty were judging the Hemingway look-alike contest.

Nick was drinking beer and watching a parade of overweight men in beards and bulky sweaters, or hunting vests, vie for the image of Key West's most famous by-product.

"Ridiculous, isn't it, Gideon?" Nick said when I came up. I had walked down here, taking my annual inventory of Duval Street.

A bear of a man with a bright nose smiled drunkenly out at the packed bar from the stage where he weaved, holding up a mug of beer before downing it in one gulp. There was hearty applause.

I agreed that it was ridiculous, but for the promoters of tourism nothing ever seemed too ridiculous. The long horseshoe bar was filled with tourists, and the tables beneath the parachute canopies and overhead fans were filled with families trying to keep some measure of control over their children who seemed to have enough sense to be bored by this contest. Nearby a group of Asians watched the proceedings with blank stares, their faces masks of incomprehension.

There were other masks, Hemingway masks, for sale at the bar, and a few people actually wandered around with a rubber likeness of Hemingway pulled over their heads.

The walls of the cavernous bar were filled with photographs and Hemingway memorabilia; lines formed at a nearby taco stand and along the counter where T-shirts were being sold with Sloppy Joe's trademark logo of Hemingway.

Jocelyn Beatty appeared and put her hand on Nick's shoulder. She smiled at me, conspiratorially it seemed, then leaned down to say something to Nick. When she was finished, she turned to me. "How goes the investigation?"

"It's getting interesting."

"Oh? Can we know?" Jocelyn's one dangling earring bobbed bewitchingly.

I wondered about the relationship between Jocelyn and Nick. They seemed closer somehow than they had the last time we were together. "They've let Sweetwater go," I said.

"Is there a new lead?"

I nodded. "Will you be at the Hemingway House tomorrow night?"

"Of course."

"It could be revealing."

"How mysterious."

I nodded. Nick, who seemed to have been listening, turned around. "You've got something, Gideon?"

"I'm not sure."

"What's that about Sweetwater?"

"He's out of jail. He'll be at the party tomorrow."

Nick smiled. "That's good news. By the way, I spoke to Maggie. She told me you went by to see her."

I nodded.

"It's okay," he said, as if I'd needed his permission. Then he turned his attention back to the stage where another look-alike was launching into a story. He had on a hunting vest with rows of slotted pockets for shotgun shells, the brass caps of several twelve-gauge shells sticking up sparkling in the stage lights. I'd had enough.

I left the bar and wandered up Duval, feeling the remote sadness brought about by the changes in the street that my people had allowed to take place for the sake of money, selling our identity in the process. It was a street owned by strangers who had converted it into a mile-long strip mall with nothing but junk being dangled like bait in front of people who probably thought this was Key West. The days when the street had been nothing but a collection of derelict bars, I thought, would always be preferable to this.

It was at such times when I most wanted to drink. Not so much to forget, but to remember. I hurried along in the heat, sweating freely, jostled by strangers, assaulted by noise, and eager to be free. I turned at the next corner. It was like stepping into a time warp. The crowds were gone. I recognized the buildings, a few of the landmarks of my youth. For a moment at least I was home again.

By the time I got back to the office I was drenched in sweat. I took off my T-shirt and carried it into the bathroom where I got a towel and began drying my body. When I came back into the office, Tom lay directly under one of the overhead fans, stretched out on his back, all four paws curled inward. The breeze rustled his whiskers and fluttered the papers on my desk.

And Asia sat in the wicker chair looking as if she'd just floated in on the tip of an iceberg.

39.

Asia was in yet another disguise. A black beret covered her hair and was pulled down low over her forehead above large, dark-lensed sunglasses. Her face was stark, except for a crimson splash of color across her lips. She looked like a star in disguise who wanted to be recognized as a star in disguise. She wore a loose-fitting tunic, bunched and belted around the waist, falling to mid-thigh. Her legs were clad in black tights. Her toes, still carrying her recent paint job, peeked through her open sandals.

"Gideon, you look tired."

"I am tired. I'm especially tired of being lied to."

Asia shifted in the chair in front of me. "Have I lied to you, Gideon?"

"What about Mickey Freeman?"

"What about him?"

"That plane you went out of here on the other night, the one you and Mickey share. You should have told me about that. Then there's a little matter of your visiting Frank that night, along with Freeman. The fact that you argued with him. It doesn't put you in a very good light right now."

"But I'm here, aren't I? I came back like you suggested."

"To turn yourself in?"

Asia's cheeks glowed. "Oh, Gideon, you don't really think I killed Frank, do you?"

"I'm open to suggestion where you and Mickey Freeman are concerned."

"I've never denied my debt to Mickey, it's just at times

you've got to move on."

"Especially when hanging around can be so uncomfort-able."

"I really did have to get back to New York for a recording session."

I stared at her.

"You don't believe me?" Her eyes misted over. "Gideon, you make it sound so sordid."

"I guess it does look that way, doesn't it? A woman like you on the way to the top caught up in a love triangle between two men like Mickey and Frank. Mickey wants to buy Frank off, but Frank can't be bought and winds up dead."

"You are just speculating, aren't you?"

"Yes, that's right, I'm just speculating. Does it strike a chord?"

"Mickey pursued me, yes."

"While you were married?"

"Yes."

"And Frank was writing about his efforts in California on behalf of Globe Oil?"

"Yes."

"Fair to say that Frank was jealous?"

"Oh, not of Mickey and me, but my success, yes."

"Well, let's see, still just speculating, of course. You and Frank argued the other night at the Hemingway House. Maybe Frank was trying to convince you to get back together instead of going through with the divorce."

Asia lowered her head. "I told you that."

"Yes, you did. But maybe he told you about Mickey trying to buy him off, the Hemingway bluff, but it wasn't working. And maybe you told Mickey. And maybe Mickey saw a way for the two of you to be rid of a major problem."

Asia looked up. "I can't believe Mickey would do some - thing like that." Her voice changed pitch, becoming almost adolescent.

I shrugged. "Did you talk to Mickey after seeing Frank?"

"Yes, but—"

"Did you tell him about Frank?"

Asia nodded slowly. "I didn't think, I mean, I didn't know that was going to happen."

"Maybe not. And maybe it didn't happen that way, but it's a possibility."

"What are you going to do?"

"I'm not going to do anything. I'm not in this anymore."

"But you still think I should go to the police?"

"That's for you to think about, not me."

"Gideon, don't be so cruel. It's just that I'm trying to avoid getting mixed up in this, having my name dragged through it."

"You're already mixed up in it. You got mixed up in it when you married Frank Maguire and had an affair with Mickey Freeman. There are reporters all over town. Why did you come back here?"

"I agreed to sing at the Hemingway House tomorrow night."

"To sing?" I was surprised. "Who asked you to do that? Mickey?"

"The director there, Ruth somebody. Mickey might have had some influence."

"Maybe you haven't moved as far away from him as you thought."

"They're paying me."

"Good. I hope they're paying you what you deserve."

Asia stood up, pouting. "You don't like me, do you, Gideon?"

"I don't know you."

When she had gone, I called Ben Kantor and told him about the break-in and the loss of Frank's notebooks.

"Who knew about them?" Kantor sounded miffed. He had every right to be.

"I don't know that anyone knew about them, but probably

a lot of people suspected their existence."

"Such as Mickey Freeman."

"From what I read, Freeman would seem to have the most to lose."

40.

The office of Senator Ira Holloway was only a few blocks from my place, part of a hideous new complex of retail establishments, pricey restaurants above which had been built a row of town houses that merely mocked the simplicity of the original architecture of our island.

A bell jangled when I opened the front door, and the young senator came out from his inner office.

"Bud, good to see you," Ira said, offering his hand. He was thirty-one years old with handsome features, a youthfully honest and tanned face. We'd met on a number of occasions when Ira, like his mentor Carl, had served as an aide in the state legislature. The last time we'd talked was at Carl's funeral.

"What brings you around?" Ira motioned me into the inner office where it was evident that the transformations of a new career were still taking place. A row of glass-fronted bookcases along one wall had been assembled and a few law books placed in them while most were still in boxes on the floor.

"I saw you at the demonstration the other day," I said. "You were talking to Mickey Freeman."

Ira smiled guilelessly. "Caught in the enemy camp." He had on a gray button-down shirt, the sleeves rolled up, a polo player charging across his chest in neat red stitching, just above his heart. "Is that what you're here about?"

I sat down in one of two burgundy leather chairs, which looked as if they'd never been sat in. I faced Ira, who perched on the edge of his desk. "I'm curious about Freeman," I said. "What do you know about him?"

"A heavy lobbyist," Ira said, grasping one knee between clasped hands. "Do you know him?"

"We've met. I hear he has an interest in buying the Hemingway House?"

"That's news to me. I didn't even know it was for sale."

I nodded. "Apparently no one outside of the place did until the murder there."

"Are you involved in that, Bud?"

"I have been."

"And you think Mickey Freeman's mixed up in it some way?"

"He knew the victim. He's been talking, maybe negotiating, with Ruth Clampitt over there. And Globe Oil's got some heavy investments around the state in the tourist industry. I'm just trying to fit the pieces together."

"I don't see how I can help you, Bud."

I shrugged. "Freeman also knew Carl. Did you know that?"

"Yes, I guess I did."

"I wonder on which side of the fence Carl sat on this oil issue."

"Well, you know offshore drilling's not popular around this state, particularly in the Keys. You're hardly going to do yourself any political favors by aligning with the oil boys."

I smiled. "But with the kind of money they've got, some of you guys seem to be able to play both ends against the middle."

"Now, Bud, that's a cynical attitude."

"And when was politics anything but cynical?"

"Well, I can tell you I'm strictly opposed to any offshore drilling."

"That sounds like a good public statement, Ira. Have you made it so strongly in private to Mickey Freeman?"

Ira stood up and ran his fingers through his thick, dark hair. "He knows where I stand." Ira went over to the bookshelf, knelt, and began taking books from the boxes and putting them on the shelves. "Was that it, Bud?"

"I suppose it was. No offense. Like I said, I'm just trying to put all these pieces together."

"None taken." But Ira didn't get up to show me out.

Leaving, I almost bumped into Freeman, who was coming along the sidewalk behind me. "Well, if it isn't Gideon Lowry paying a call on his representative. It's good to see participatory government in action."

"I hear you're pretty good at it yourself. Maybe I should take a lesson. Have you got a minute?"

Mickey looked at the door to Ira Holloway's, turned back to me, and smiled. "Of course I have, pardner. Let me buy you a drink."

A few doors down was a bar in a restaurant and we went in there. It was the first time I'd been at a bar in several weeks except for when I was working. I asked for a club soda. Mickey ordered Canadian Club on the rocks.

"You don't drink?" he asked.

"I'm a drunk."

He shook his head and lifted his glass. "To those who have learned how to live with themselves."

I took a sip of club soda. "Do you think that's something Frank Maguire had learned?"

Mickey Freeman smiled and lit a cigarette. "Frank was slow, but he had real possibilities."

"And you were teaching him."

Mickey shook his head. "We all have something to teach each other."

"I understand you were, or are, negotiating to buy the Hemingway House. Frank was going to become its occupant, the writer in residence."

Mickey looked at me over the rim of his glass as he drank. "Who would have thought a town this small would have been able to hold on to a pit bull like you."

"I was born here. We're simple island people, but we've

always been able to spot grifters when we see them."

"Aren't you lucky."

"No, probably not. Mostly just determined, I would say."

"Well, you might want to get determined with someone else. There's no percentage in pursuing me."

"How many trips did you and Maguire take to Cuba?"

Mickey spilled his drink on the bar. "Where'd you hear that?"

"Frank wrote about it. Filled up several notebooks in fact. You never saw those notebooks?"

Mickey shook his head, wiping his mouth with a napkin as the bartender cleaned up the spilled drink and put a fresh one on a mat in front of him.

"All brightly colored," I said. "You couldn't miss them."

"I don't remember any notebooks."

"That's funny, because I had them on my desk the other day and last night somebody came in and took them."

"You don't say."

"I had to wonder who might have the most to lose by seeing their contents made public. Guess whose name came up on my short list?"

"I'm no good at guessing games. Too much chance involved."

"You didn't really think you were buying his silence, did you?"

"I don't know what you're talking about."

"And you don't want to account for your whereabouts about one o'clock this morning. Or after midnight the night Maguire was killed."

"No, and I don't think I have to!"

"Maybe not in the past, but from where I sit the rules are different."

"Then maybe it's time for you to change seats." Mickey drained his glass, put a ten-dollar bill on the bar, and walked out. I looked around at the decor, listened to the elevator music coming from the piano player, and got up and left in search of some place in the lower-rent district for dinner.

41.

After dinner I sat at my desk and watched the evening fall prey to the night. Duval Street, practically empty, seemed haunted as the flickering gray streetlamps came on at dusk. I had off the next two nights at the Pier House, and as the night invaded, I sat in the dark. Metaphorically as well as literally. I leaned back in my chair, content to remain hidden, lost as I was, as though daylight might never again reach me.

I watched as someone came up on the porch, peered into the glass, and rapped once on the door.

"It's open," I shouted.

"Bud, what are you doing sitting in here in the dark?"

I recognized George Lewis's voice as he came in and stood just inside the door. I reached forward and pulled the chain on the desk lamp, blinking against the sudden intrusion.

"Thinking," I said. "Care to join me?"

George sat down. "The Maguire case?"

"Among others," I lied. Unless I counted the anonymous notes Nick Farr had begun receiving again, there were no other cases, and Nick had not hired me on any official basis.

"Anything shaking?" George asked.

I regarded George across the desk from me with some amusement. A few days ago he was practically ready to haul me in for obstructing justice. Now he was all conciliatory, full of cheerful bonhomie, in the wake, no doubt, of his own failures.

"What's wrong, your investigation stalled?"

George smiled. "I talked to your nonclient. She's something, isn't she?"

"Asia?" I shook my head. "I take it you didn't get much out of her."

George snorted. "She's loony. Kept telling me what a human angel I was. I would ask her a question and get three back in reply. Half the time I never knew where she was going. You have that experience?"

"Asia's different."

"You want to know what I think?"

Probably not, but I didn't say so.

"I think she's guilty as sin."

"Did you haul her in?" I asked with undisguised sarcasm.

"Bud, go easy. Sweetwater was one of the last people to see Maguire alive. I had hoped we'd be able to get something out of him, but I knew we'd only do it by bringing him in. He wouldn't even have talked about fighting with Maguire if we hadn't scared him into it. You know that. Sweetwater's as closemouthed as you are."

I shrugged. "What's that got to do with Asia?"

George smiled slyly. "Maybe if you'd told me about her when I asked you, I wouldn't have had to put the squeeze on Sweetwater."

"So you really think she killed him."

"I think she could have. I think she could do just about anything she wanted and walk away from it like it was just a sad mess on the street. Something to step over and move on."

"She told you about Maguire?"

"You mean the business of the divorce, wanting to give him a settlement?"

I nodded.

"Yeah, she said something about that. And I believed it about as much as I believe pigs can fly."

I watched a trail of ants cross my desktop in single file.

"People get divorced," I said. "Some even pay for the pleasure."

"Sure, but not this one, not fifty grand in one pile to a man who could make twice that without breaking a sweat."

"Who told you that?"

"The one who was married to a Hemingway. Jocelyn what's her name. Don't tell me you don't know about her?"

"Maguire was writing a book from a Hemingway manuscript she'd given him."

"Right, and a publisher had made an offer of a hundred grand."

"I didn't know that."

"But they turned it down. They were going to let the book go to auction. You know what that means?"

"Tell me." George was clearly impressed with himself. A small-town cop grappling with the sophisticated world normally outside his ken. I didn't want to spoil any fun for him.

"They would let several different publishers take a look at it, then bid on it. The highest bidder got it. Jocelyn expected it to go in excess of two hundred thousand. Maybe as high as half a million. We're talking a new Hemingway book here."

"I'm impressed. But whoever turned down fifty thousand dollars just because they were making money."

"I didn't say Maguire would turn it down. I never thought it was a legitimate offer in the first place."

"So what do you figure Asia wanted?"

"She wanted you to find Maguire. Do the hard work for her. The rest she could handle on her own."

"Neat. You've wrapped it all up. Now you mind telling me why she killed him?"

George smiled. "You're an all-take, no-give kind of guy, Bud. I was hoping you might have something to contribute along that line."

I wondered if I did. Asia. The possibility had never been far from my mind. Especially with the Mickey Freeman connection.

"Did you check out Mickey Freeman?"

"Of course I did, Bud, of course I did. You think we don't

know what we're doing downtown? You're the only real detective around here? Interesting guy, Freeman. Lot of connections."

"None hopefully that prevented you from asking him the tough questions."

George ignored the innuendo. "Well, so far the only real link we've got is that plane Asia flew out of here on. One of those little things you thought I didn't need to know." George tugged at his earlobe.

"I was protecting my client."

"Who may be a murderer."

"I'm not convinced of that. You want to give me something more concrete than supposition, I'll be happy to reconsider that opinion, but right now I stand by it."

George moved his hand from his ear to his nose, pinching the nostrils between thumb and forefinger while clearing his throat. "Bud, where did you learn all those big words?"

"From my mother. She studied Latin and was proud of her vocabulary."

George shifted uneasily in his seat. My people had never been comfortable with too much education. He changed the subject. "There's a personal connection between Freeman and Asia."

"Sure, but it was ancient history. And besides Maguire wasn't exactly standing in the way of her other relationships."

"How do you know?"

"I talked to Asia and I talked to Maguire. Neither one of them suggested that was a problem."

"So she just wanted a divorce and thought she had to buy her way out of it."

"Or wanted to because of some past commitment."

George shook his head. "I don't think so."

I shrugged.

"If that was the case," George said, "what were they fighting about at the party that night? Plenty of people witnessed that."

"Maguire was drunk. He was giving everyone a hard time."

"But I hear he was trying to talk her out of going through with the divorce. He wanted her back."

"Asia told you that?"

George nodded. "She said she told you, too."

Yes, and it had nagged at me at the time. And perhaps I'd been too taken with Asia and too put off by Maguire to pursue it the way I should have. "How did she get her hands on the gun?"

"Maybe she didn't. Maybe she hired someone to do it for her. She could get somebody for five grand, which is forty-five less than she said she was willing to pay for a no-fault divorce."

I shook my head. "I don't buy it. Asia might be ambitious, but she isn't crazy enough to risk her career over a guy who isn't hurting her."

George stared up at the ceiling for a moment. "You still like Mickey Freeman, don't you?"

"He's still got the most to lose."

"And how do you intend to prove it?"

"I don't know. I'm open to suggestion."

"Sweetwater," George said quietly.

"What?"

"What if he saw something that night that would identify the killer?"

"He didn't."

George winked. "But only you and I know that. The killer doesn't know it."

After George left, I went for a walk. The night air was redolent of the past, suffused with a kind of tepid sweetness, the scent of jasmine hanging over half-deserted streets. In my mind I could still hear George Lewis's voice hammering away at Asia while I tried to defend her, a defense that became weaker and weaker as her association with Mickey Freeman grew more complex. Even if she wasn't directly guilty of Frank's murder, I had to admit it now seemed more and more likely that she would have had knowledge of it.

42.

Early the next morning I rode my bike down to the pier for sunrise, then returned home and fed Tom. After a shower and a shave, I put on a fresh pair of khakis and a clean T-shirt before going for breakfast at the drugstore where I bought a paper and sat at the counter beside Sweetwater.

"Bud, they asked me to come back and referee the fight tonight."

"I thought they might." Adding sugar to my coffee, I didn't look at Sweets. "You seen George Lewis recently?"

"No, sir. Seen all I want to see of that man for a while."

I pulled out the Keys section of the *Miami Herald*. Today was Hemingway's birthday. A detailed article described the culmination of the week-long festival, then recounted the tragic death at the Hemingway House almost a week ago. For the first time much was made of Asia's relationship to the victim, and according to George Lewis, the police were following up a substantial lead from a possible witness. They hoped to make an arrest soon. The rest of the information was old news, but I read it slowly anyway.

When my breakfast came, Sweets, who had finished eating, stood up to leave. "Hope I see you there tonight," he said.

"I'll be there."

He nodded. I stared into his lined, worn face that gave not a clue as to what was going on behind his dark eyes. "Something troubling you, Bud?"

"Sweets—" I began.

"Yes, Bud?"

"Ah, nothing. Good luck tonight. I'm in your corner."

Sweetwater grinned and walked away.

I was troubled. Troubled by what George was doing, the jeopardy into which Sweetwater was being placed. And I was troubled by what to do about it, whether to warn Sweets and risk the possibility that he might decide not to come tonight, or to say nothing and just be there myself and provide what security I could. Because in my mind I'd already decided that George's strategy could be worth the risk. Which made me feel as if I'd already betrayed Sweetwater.

When I got home, a message from Jocelyn was on the answering machine. I sat down at my desk and dialed her number. When she answered, her voice was cool and distant, and I pictured her out on the balcony of her time-share with a cordless phone, her clothes crisp and well tailored and her eyes with that intense stare as she surveyed the harbor.

"Nick told me about the notes he's been getting," Jocelyn said.

"Has he gotten another one?"

"Yes. Three words printed on a piece of paper. It said, 'Tonight's the night.'"

Bang, bang, you're next. And, *tonight's the night.* If it was a hoax, the timing was perfect to put the fear of God into Nick, I thought. If it wasn't a hoax ... I didn't finish the thought. Jocelyn said, "I see in the paper the police have a lead."

"Yes, and whoever killed Maguire must have seen it, too. The Hemingway House might be the safest place for anyone to be tonight. Has Nick reported this to the police yet?"

"No, he doesn't want to do that. He doesn't think they can do anything and that it will just create more problems than it will solve. He said you had worked on this a few months ago when he was getting these."

"The notes then weren't quite so specific. I think he should go to the police. Especially since there is a possible link with Maguire's death. Is Nick going to finish the Hemingway book

Maguire started?"

"Yes, I've asked him to."

"Then it could be no coincidence that he's getting threatening notes. By not handing them over to the police he's impeding an investigation."

"You should tell him."

"I will."

When we hung up, I called Nick. "Jocelyn just told me you received another note."

Nick tried to laugh it off. "Some crank."

I didn't buy it. "Then you haven't been to the police."

"I'm thinking about it."

"What's there to think about?"

"You know how this stuff works. Once it goes public, I'm a target for every crazy in town."

"What if it's not a crank but Maguire's killer?"

"It sounds a little too opportunistic."

"But if it isn't? What about Maggie?"

"She's worried. I can't do anything about that."

"Do you want her back?"

Nick hesitated. "Why do you ask?"

"Because it occurred to me that getting her sympathy might not be a bad way to go about it."

"I'm going to ignore that in the interest of our friendship."

"Do that. It was just a thought. Jocelyn says you're finishing the Hemingway book."

"Right. I've taken on another project."

"Congratulations. Are you going to the party tonight?"

"I'll be there." Nick sounded remote. "I'll keep my distance from the pool house."

"George Lewis thinks he's on to something. Your information might be helpful. You might want to check with a lawyer. You could be breaking the law by withholding it."

Nick was silent for a moment. "I'll think about it. If I go to Lewis, can I trust him to keep it out of the papers?"

"I think so."

We hung up and I spent the morning knocking around the house, doing idle work. I fixed one of the loose panels in the hardwood floor in the office and sorted through the file cabinets disposing of old files. Just busywork done mostly to keep from thinking. I was nervous, biding my time, and skittish as a sparrow hawk in a windstorm.

A few minutes before one I was in the kitchen putting out some fresh water for Tom when there was a knock on the front door. I walked into the office. Casey stood framed in the glass, holding up her hand in a familiar wave. She was alone.

43.

At Casey's request we lunched at Louie's, sitting on the deck overlooking the Atlantic. Although it hadn't been that long since I'd last seen her, it seemed like another lifetime ago, so much had changed. Casey looked good; she had cut her hair short so that it fluffed around her face making it seem fuller, and the age lines were neatly softened behind makeup. Her eyes were questioning, and she smiled brightly.

"You look good," I said. "Miami seems to agree with you."

"It's exciting. I feel like I'm doing something with my life for a change."

I nodded understandingly. Casey had escaped the rut that Key West could become for a woman who wanted more out of life than just survival. Mere existence. And who could begrudge her that? But there was something sadly dispiriting, I thought, for those of us left behind, remaining here like caretakers, as though we were guardians for those with motivation enough to escape this island.

"And you've found love?"

"Oh, Bud, I don't know. I'm not even questioning that right now." She reached her hand across the table and took mine. "How are you doing?"

I knew she was not asking about my general condition in life, but the one galvanizing theme that was central to her own existence. "I haven't had a drink since before you left," I said.

Casey studied me without saying anything.

"It hasn't been easy. There have been times when getting a drink has been the sole occupation of my thoughts for a day or two at a time. But I've managed to beat it."

"Good for you, Bud. I'm proud of you, but it isn't over."

"According to you it will never be over. One day at a time."

Casey smiled. "It's hell, isn't it?"

"More like purgatory."

We ordered lunch and then talked about the murder at the Hemingway House. Casey was fascinated that I knew Asia, had actually played the piano while she sang. That seemed to interest her more than the fact that Asia had been married to Frank Maguire, now dead.

"What's she like?" Casey asked.

I thought of George Lewis's description: *guilty as sin*. It didn't fit the Asia that I knew. But perhaps that was because I didn't want it to fit. "I think she's a little scared of her own success. She hasn't really found an identity yet."

"I hear she's singing tonight."

"Yes, are you going to be there?"

Casey nodded. "I'd like to meet her."

I couldn't imagine why. Casey was in her forties, long past the starstruck years, and Asia seemed, to me at least, generational. However, I did agree to try to introduce them.

We ate and talked about Key West, what had happened here since she left, which wasn't much, and Casey's life in Miami. Where she lived, what her job was like, the people she knew. By the time we had finished, it was clear that despite our affection for one another, a gulf was now between us as distinct as if we inhabited different planets. For me, Miami was a foreign country. I could no more imagine living in that city than I could in Paris or Rome. I was rooted to this patch of rock in the middle of the ocean in a way that was beyond a simple choice of where to live. I clung to my ancestral domain, the habits of the generations, the way Catholic sinners abided mass. It was a place of refuge in a world of upheaval.

When Casey dropped me back home in her car and we said good-bye, it was with the knowledge that a subtle shift had taken place in our relationship, that we were like strangers who have met on a train, now once again back at our real destinations. The interlude had been fun, but it was finished. From here on it was Christmas cards, and a few phone calls that would diminish in frequency.

There was a message on the answering machine to call George Lewis. Urgent. I sat down on the edge of the desk, still wearing the dark glasses I'd hidden behind while at lunch with Casey. I felt a sense of loss, weary. I dialed George, who picked up on the second ring.

"I had an interesting talk with your buddy Nick Farr," George said.

So Nick had taken my advice. "About the letters?"

"Yeah. Another thing you failed to tell me about."

"It was Nick's call. He wanted to avoid the publicity. And until yesterday none of those notes related to the Maguire murder."

"Well, they sure as hell do now. This puts a whole new pitch on the case."

I thought about the issue I'd raised with Nick earlier, the idea that these notes could have been a way to get back with Maggie. "Did he tell you he'd gotten some anonymous notes a few months ago?"

"Yeah, except they didn't threaten his life."

"No, but the format was the same. I had no luck finding out who was behind it. After a few weeks when they stopped coming, Nick forgot it."

"Did you turn anything up?"

"We assumed it was a woman. Nick had taught a writing course in Miami some weeks before the notes started up. There'd been a flirtation with one of the women in the course, but nothing came of it. I tried to track her down without success."

"If these are legit, this is more than a jilted romance!"

"There may be no connection between the two."

"Which still leaves the real possibility that there's a geek out there who's got it in for writers or Hemingway or writers who write about Hemingway."

"What's Nick going to do?"

"I know only one thing he's not going to do and that's to show up at that party tonight."

I hung up, got on my bike, and called on Jocelyn at her time-share.

44.

Jocelyn opened the door when I rang, inviting me in. All available space in the living room seemed filled with Hemingway's image. There were books, T-shirts, posters, and masks. Souvenir beer mugs and ashtrays. The middle of the floor was surrounded with manuscripts. Jocelyn, in shorts and an overlarge T-shirt with Papa's bearded face staring out at me, looked somewhat bewildered by it all.

"Thank God, it's over. The end." She collapsed in an elegant pile on the floor in among the manuscripts, putting her hand on a stack of paper. "Short stories. Nearly six hundred of them."

"You've read them all?"

"At least the first page." She tried to smile. Her face was tense, lines etched at the corners of her mouth. "It's been a grueling week. Sit down if you can find a place."

I straddled the armrest of a chair. "You must get some real nuts in these contests."

"A few I suppose."

"You ever meet them?"

Jocelyn shook her head. "They come from all over the States. There's a writers' workshop and some of the people who submitted stories take part in that. I might meet the writer of the winning story. That's about it."

"You come across anything exceptionally weird in this year's crop?"

"You mean someone who could kill a writer like Frank, or Nick?"

I nodded. It seemed as probable as any other lead. Perhaps the person who had been in Nick's course had also entered this contest. If so, it would mean checking six hundred names against the names in Nick's class, if he still had access to them—not an enormous task, but one that was beset with time constraints if it proved correct and we were to find whoever it was between now and tonight's party.

"There were plenty of bad stories, badly written," Jocelyn said, "but I can't think of any that struck me as psychotic."

"How difficult a task would it be to get the list of names of the contestants?"

"The judges never see the names, but the organizers have them." She stood up and went over to a table where the phone was and made a call. She spoke for a few minutes, then came back to her place on the floor. "You can pick up the list of names at their office next to Sloppy Joe's."

"Mind if I use your phone?"

Jocelyn motioned with a help-yourself gesture.

I called Nick. "Do you still have that list of names of the students who took your writing course a few months ago?" I asked when he answered.

"Probably somewhere, if I can find it."

"Do your best and bring it down to the chief of detectives at the police department. I'll meet you down there in twenty minutes."

I hung up and went to the door. "Do you know the winner yet?"

"It's between two stories. I'm meeting with the other judges later. I don't think there will be much of a controversy."

"You won't make the announcement public for a while, will you?"

"Not until tonight," Jocelyn smiled distantly as I went out the door.

Fifteen minutes later I sat in George Lewis's office with six hundred names, along with Nick Farr and his list of twenty-four, and explained my theory to George. "We check these two lists, and if any of the names overlap, you can run a computer check. It's a shot in the dark."

George grunted. "Sounds more like a wild-goose chase to me."

"What have we got to lose?"

"Nothing except time."

"If you run some photocopies, we can break it down and divide the work up."

George took the lists and went out of the office, returning moments later with two sets of photocopies. The three of us took two hundred names each from the long list and began checking them against Nick's list. There was no sound except the shifting of paper. Once the phone rang. George switched off the bell.

Less than half an hour later, I came across a name that was vaguely familiar—from the time when I'd seen Nick's list several months ago. "Tim Wannamaker," I said.

"On both lists?" George asked.

"Right here." I pushed the two lists across the desk. The address was a post office box in Miami. There was also the title of his short story entry: "Rain Delay."

"Ring a bell?" I asked Nick.

"The name's familiar. I'm not sure I can put a face to it, though."

George picked up the phone and relayed Wannamaker's name to be plugged into the computer in case he was wanted for anything. I stood up. Nick studied the lists as though he were looking for another match of names.

When George got off the phone, I asked to use it and called Jocelyn. "Do you remember a story called 'Rain Delay'?" I asked when she answered.

"It's the story I think is going to win."

"You're kidding." I repeated what she said to Nick and George. "What's it about?" I asked her.

A divorced father, she explained, who takes his son to a baseball game. The game is delayed because of rain. The father and son talk while sitting under an umbrella. The son reveals that his mother is getting married and they are probably going to move to another city. The effect this news has on the father was the basis of the story.

"Nothing startling there," I said when Jocelyn finished.

"It was very well written. Don't tell me the writer's the one you are looking for?"

"He might be."

There was a knock on George's door and a secretary came in and passed a computer printout to George. "Nothing on Tim Wannamaker," she said.

"Shit. This could take some time then," George said. "We can try to track him down via his address with the help of the Miami police. But don't expect miracles. Until then, about all we can do is keep our fingers crossed."

I nodded. Nick stood up. I looked at my watch. It was less than two hours until the party would begin at the Hemingway House. I held up crossed fingers and left.

45.

Nick followed me out of George's office and we stood outside on the buckled sidewalk beneath the royal poinciana tree. The heat was oppressive, weighted, a deathly stillness in the air. Nick ran a hand through his rumpled hair, his shirt already sweat-stained. An old hulk of a car went by, its body custom-painted in a garish tropical scene with palm trees, dogs, and along one front side panel a sailboat beating across the horizon.

"Tim Wannamaker," Nick said, watching the progress of the car as it sputtered along Angela Street. "I'm trying to get a picture of him. It was only a few months ago. There were a couple of guys in the class, one of them real quiet. I think it might have been Wannamaker."

"What did he look like, Nick?"

"Lanky, bland. Nothing distinguishing except that he never said much."

"Did he write anything?"

"He must have. It was a requirement for the course, but I don't remember his particular work."

"Jocelyn says the story is good. Very good."

"What's it called?"

"'Rain Delay.' About a father who takes his kid to a ball game and finds out his ex-wife is moving to another city with another man, taking the kid."

"Sounds familiar." Nick shook his head. "I might have read something like that."

"Wannamaker could have been working on 'Rain Delay'

182

then and submitted it for the Hemingway contest. Maybe you criticized it. Came down hard on the kid. Was he a kid?"

"Yeah, if it's the same guy." Nick laughed. "So I inspired him. He wins the contest and gets even with his instructor."

"Would you recognize Wannamaker if you saw him?"

"I think so." Nick kicked a pebble out into the street. "But why would Wannamaker want to kill Maguire? That doesn't make sense."

"It's possible, if it is Wannamaker who's threatening you, that he's using the Maguire killing for his own cover."

"But George Lewis suggested there was a witness."

"Yeah, Sweetwater."

"Sweetwater? He saw Maguire's killer?"

"He may have seen something at a distance. Lewis is hoping to flush whoever it is out." A pair of sparrow hawks screeched as they wheeled across the treetops. "George said you aren't coming tonight."

Nick shrugged. "Since I'm the one Wannamaker wants and the only person who might be able to identify him, I guess I should be there."

I unlocked my bike from the rack. "I'll see you in a couple of hours then. And don't worry, you're going to have plenty of protection."

Nick didn't look overly confident, but he waved and walked up the street.

I rode home and found Dan Riggs sitting in the swing on my porch, reading a paper and drinking from a Styrofoam cup. A small canvas backpack lay beside him on the swing. "Mr. Lowry, I just got here. Thought I'd sit a minute and wait for you."

"Nothing better to do?"

"Well, things are coming together now that you mention it." Riggs seemed excited by something. On edge.

"Do tell." I opened the door and invited him inside.

"I saw Mickey Freeman."

"Did you now? How does he look?"

"He looked fine, but that was probably because of the woman he was having breakfast with. I thought you'd like to know about it." Riggs idly stroked one end of his mustache, like an arch villain in an old silent movie.

"You probably want to give me three guesses and the first two won't count."

"Well, it was Asia. You knew?"

"Let's say I'm not surprised. Why should you be? They know each other, have for years. They ought to be able to have breakfast without setting off any alarms."

Riggs smiled as though he'd just baited a trap. "Listen to this."

"I'm all ears."

"While they were eating, I went by his room. The door was open and a maid was cleaning the bathroom. I went in, told her I'd forgotten something, and took a look around."

"The job security for detectives is suddenly looking questionable..."

Riggs grinned, reaching for his backpack next to him. "Investigative reporters and detectives have got a lot in common." He opened the flap on the pack and took out several brightly colored notebooks. "Recognize these?"

I nodded, running my hand over the bump on the back of my head, which was diminishing gradually.

"Interesting reading. *Rolling Stone* will be glad to see them." Riggs pushed them back in the knapsack and stood up. "I thought you ought to know. In case it makes any difference to the rest of your investigation."

When he had gone, I showered and shaved. The phone rang while I was shaving. I got to it on the third ring and heard George Lewis's voice on the other end. "Wannamaker is dead."

"What!"

"Killed in a car accident some months back."

"What about the story he wrote? When did that arrive?"

184

"Ironically, a couple days after the accident."

"Jesus."

"Yeah, like I said earlier, this is turning into a real crap-shoot."

After hanging up, I went in and dressed, then came back and sat behind the desk. In the far corner of the room, near the ceiling, a cobweb fluttered in the light breeze from the overhead fan. I watched it for a moment before opening the desk drawer and reaching into the back to take out Captain Billy's revolver. The bone grips felt smooth and cool. I found a box of shells and took out six blunt-nosed bullets. They felt heavy in my hand as I opened the breech, filled the six chambers of the revolver, snapping the cylinder closed when I was done.

The gun weighed me down, immobilized me in a way I could never explain. I stared at the instrument of death, the same way Captain Billy and Carl must have stared at it moments before they ended their lives. I tried to imagine the sound it would make, the shock in my hand as it went off, and realized how unsure I was that I could even pull the trigger.

Here was my history, my legacy, and it belonged buried along with its previous owners, but for some morbid reason I had chosen to keep it, the one memento mori from the Lowry family that I could not escape. I stood up from the desk, my legs weak, and looked down at Tom, who had come in from the kitchen and now stood in the middle of the floor staring up at me, as though questioning my actions. I slid the gun into the waistband of my khakis and callously donned a seldom-worn sport coat to help conceal it.

46.

I walked the few blocks to the Hemingway House, sweating freely so that by the time I got there the light jacket was limp. Wallace, at his post, sneered when he saw me come in. "If it isn't the bad penny!"

"Looks like you're going to have some competition tonight."

"What's that supposed to mean?"

"The Hemingway look-alikes. They'll be all over the place."

"Who said I was competing?"

"I'm told you've been competing ever since you went to work here. You see yourself as some sort of incarnation of the place, the spirit of Hemingway maybe."

"That's sick," Wallace said, his voice rising even higher than its normally high pitch.

"Probably. When you're in the house here alone at night, what do you do, write?"

Wallace looked at me as if I'd caught him with his hand in the cookie jar. "I told you I wasn't in there that night."

"Someone was, or the lights wouldn't have been on. You were the last to leave. You wouldn't have left the lights on, would you?"

Wallace ran a hand over his bearded face. Something shifted in his eyes. He looked trapped.

"You know you could be an accessory if you're withholding information, don't you?"

"Listen, I've told the police everything I know. I don't have to answer any more of your questions."

"Okay," I said, stepping around him. "Let me find George Lewis and make it official."

People were moving in through the gate. "I don't have time for this now."

"Later, then." I winked and moved on. The grounds of the Hemingway House were floodlit with fairy lights strung through the palm trees. The interior of the house was also lit, but closed to the public, and the crowd roamed the grounds, gathering near the two bars set up by the pool.

The ring was in the back, shrouded in darkness with red, white, and blue bunting cascading to the ground from its deck around all four sides. Bleachers stood on one side of the ring. Posters of Hemingway and T-shirts with his image were for sale nearby at a long table.

"Reduced to a poster boy," Nick Farr said, coming up beside me. "I wonder if it would make the old boy laugh or cry."

"Who gets all the royalties?"

"Some scab the closest he got to a book was reading the graffiti on the wall in the men's room." Nick smiled. "Any news?"

"Wannamaker was killed in a car wreck." I told him what George Lewis had passed along.

Nick shifted from foot to foot uneasily. "What about the story?"

"Either the connection we made with Wannamaker is co-incidence, or someone's using Wannamaker's name to conceal his own identity."

Nick stared into the darkness of the ring. "Where does that leave me?"

I shrugged. "In the dark, along with the rest of us."

From the side yard the sound of a band struck up a calypso beat. A woman's voice, sounding much like a young Rosemary Clooney, sang, "C'mon a my house, c'mon."

I walked around there. A small platform stage had been erected with some scaffolding around it that held several colored spotlights. The band was a five-piece combo with someone on trumpet, trombone, drums, rhythm guitar, and keyboard. Asia, at the forefront of the stage, was in a red, fringed dress cut just above her knees, and red high heels. The dress shimmered in the light as she swayed to the music. She segued into "I'm a Redhot Mama," growling the lyrics into a handheld mike as she pranced across the stage.

I stood in the shadows of one darkened corner of the house surveying the crowd. A hundred or more people stood in the side yard watching, applauding. Many of them had on Hemingway T-shirts; some even wore the rubber Hemingway masks I'd seen around town. It was an energetic crowd, everyone carrying plastic drink containers, and it was growing. Party time. I saw a couple of cops moving along the inside of the wall opposite me and wondered if George had briefed them on what, or who, they were looking for.

"Love for Sale." Asia slowed the tempo down as I walked around to the front of the house where Wallace reigned over the entrance as more people crowded inside. I saw Ben Kantor and went over to him.

"*Rolling Stone*'s got the Maguire notebooks," I said.

He turned, startled. "You jest."

"Their reporter was snooping and found them in Freeman's room."

"Have you talked to him, Freeman?"

"Not yet. I just learned about it this evening."

"It puts him in a compromising position, doesn't it?"

"It might have if he still had the notebooks, but since he doesn't, there's not much anyone can do. *Rolling Stone*'s not likely to let them go or leak their contents, at least until they've had a chance to look over them."

Kantor was in a seersucker suit with sweat stains showing beneath the arms. "So my story has been scooped."

"It looks that way."

Kantor shook his head. I wasn't sure if he was angry or disappointed by the loss of the story because it was hard to measure just how personally involved he'd been in the Globe Oil investigation. Perhaps, after Maguire's murder, Kantor had decided that the stakes were too high. He smiled tightly and wandered off.

I walked around to the back feeling acutely self-conscious, aware of each step I took and the unyielding burden welded to my waist like a malignant growth. As a kid I had played around here a few times when I'd accompanied my mother, who was visiting Pauline. I could never have imagined then that this residence would have attracted the kind of crowds that we saw now. Then it was just another house, like many others in Key West, and its main attraction, for me at least, was the swimming pool, at the time the only pool in town.

I found Sweetwater, wearing an undershirt tucked into his dark slacks, in the changing room, hanging up a starched and freshly ironed white shirt. He grinned when I came in. I noticed that the door to the storage room now had a hasp and lock on it. I talked for a while with Sweetwater, feeling weak in the legs, as sweat beaded on my forehead.

"You okay, Bud?"

"I'll be fine." I rubbed the back of my hand across my brow. "Listen, Sweets, be careful tonight."

"Oh, you can be sure, Bud. Ain't gonna be no trouble from this quarter."

I leaned against the wall for a moment and watched Sweetwater check out the fight equipment on the table. He moved around, examining each item, holding the gloves in his hands with a certain reverence. I stepped outside.

The grounds were now jammed with people. Ruth Clampitt was just turning away from one of her staff, about to return to her office. She saw me and said, "Are you satisfied?"

"That you brought Sweetwater back?" I shrugged. "He's the closest link to Hemingway that you've got around here. Market him right and he'll put money in the till. Or maybe you don't care about that anymore."

"I care about running a successful business. What makes you think I wouldn't?" Ruth had on a purple tunic dress with lots of pleats and folds that hid her ample figure.

"Well, I was thinking maybe the place had been sold. Or maybe Mickey Freeman had backed out of the negotiations."

Ruth's painted eyebrows arched above her sequined glasses. "What is that supposed to mean?"

"I think Mickey Freeman was pressuring you to sell this place, maybe even making an offer it would be difficult to refuse, and you wanted to refuse it. Wallace might think you're not running this place right, but it's crawling with people. You're sitting on a gold mine here."

Ruth smiled. "I'm glad you think so."

"I think so. But Freeman was a hard man to refuse. He gets around, Mickey does. He's got his hand in a lot of different projects around the state. I wonder if you ever came across him when you were on the west coast running museums there?"

Ruth glanced around at the crowd now beginning to spread across the grounds.

"Maybe Mickey was an investor here early on. Maybe instead of buying the place he already had a sufficient share to encourage you to put Frank Maguire in here as a way of getting Frank off his back. And maybe you tried to argue Mickey out of that idea since it might hamper operations here, slow down the revenues. Once Frank was dead, however, Mickey would lose interest. And the pressure would be off you."

"I hope you're not suggesting what I think you're suggesting."

I shrugged. "But you can see why I might think that, can't you?"

Ruth sighed. "All right, Mickey wanted to put Maguire in the writing studio, let him live and work there. I thought it was a terrible idea, but I didn't kill Frank Maguire if that's what you're getting at."

John Leslie

I wasn't getting at anything. I was thinking out loud, hoping I could get a spark, and apparently I had. Ruth seemed tentative, on the verge of saying something more, but before she could she was interrupted by a staff person who needed her, and Ruth moved away to deal with another problem.

I went to the bar and asked for a club soda and tried to quench my thirst and ease the fevered tension that I felt hanging in the air like a stalled weather front.

47.

A spotlight was turned on above the ring when I ambled over to the bleachers and stood where I could have a clear view of the fights and the spectators. Moments later Sweetwater climbed into the ring. He wore a long-sleeved white shirt, the sleeves an inch too short for his arms, the collar frayed and buttoned at his neck. He had on dark slacks and a pair of tennis shoes. And as he walked around the ring checking the equipment, Sweets nodded once in my direction.

Music blared from a loudspeaker as I watched the parade of costumes while the bleachers began to fill with media and spectators, most of whom I didn't recognize. They were young, many of them tourists, I guessed, and the professional partiers who never missed an event.

Ten minutes passed before the three judges for the fight took their places at a table at one end of the ring, and a few minutes later the floodlights went off and the music died, leaving the ring in darkness once again. The crowd settled into a restless silence before a disembodied voice came over the loudspeaker: "Ladieees and gentleeemen." The spotlight was turned on the ring. Sweetwater stood in one corner, his long arms outstretched, his hands gripping the uppermost ring ropes, his face a mask of impassivity. In the center of the ring, wearing a tuxedo and holding a microphone, was a short-haired blond woman, a broad grin on her face. "Welcome," she said in the same exaggerated growling voice, "to the first annual Hemingway Boxing Tournament." A cheer went up from the crowd.

I listened absently to the preamble and introductions while keeping my eyes on the crowd. When the ring announcer introduced Sweetwater, "a man who sparred with Hemingway and lived to tell about it," Sweets came to the center of the ring lifting his hands above his head. Flashbulbs were going off all around us.

"Jesus," a guy beside me said as the crowd applauded, "where do they find these guys?"

"He's legit," I said.

"You know him?"

I nodded and the guy wandered away. After a few more remarks by the ring announcer, the first contestants were introduced—a black kid whose family name I recognized and a Hispanic kid I'd never heard of. The black kid's trunks were too big for him and he wore torn sneakers, while the Hispanic was decked out in regulation shoes and designer trunks. Sweetwater brought them to the center of the ring and gave them their instructions. They touched gloves before going to their corners where a trainer gave each boy a last-minute pep talk and inserted a mouthpiece between his teeth. The bell sounded and they came out nervously punching air.

It was a three-round fight with the black kid dominating the final two rounds, scoring heavily with a flurry of combination punches and quick footwork that left his opponent backed against the ropes, his hands held defensively in front of his face. I watched Sweetwater, whose own footwork belied his age, although within seconds of the first round, large sweat stains darkened his white shirt. He was quick to separate the boxers, and watching him work brought back memories of Captain Billy, who had taught me to box in the backyard of our William Street home where a heavy bag hung from a limb of the sapodilla tree that shaded the yard against the heat of tropical summer days. The smack of the gloves, sweat glistening on the boys' bodies, reminded me of those somnolent afternoons when I was always aware that Phyllis watched disapprovingly from the screened-in Florida room while the captain stood behind the bag, shouting instructions like a drill sergeant.

Sweetwater hovered in those memories, always on the edge, like a dark frigate bird riding the air currents of the summer sky. I heard his voice resounding in the black choir of the church that was within a few blocks of our home, and, of course, at the funerals where he followed the black band that marked the passage of time, beating out the cadence on a bass drum.

I was lost in a reverie, taken back in time as I watched Sweetwater, unaware of anyone next to me, when a voice said, "Bud?"

I turned. It was George Lewis. "You okay, Bud?"

"Yeah, fine. What have you got?"

"The Wannamaker connection. We located his parents, who live in a little town near Spokane, Washington. Tim was their youngest son; an older one died last year of AIDS. It was a close family. The parents are still devastated."

"How old was Tim?"

"He was in his last year of college. He wanted to be a writer."

"Had he said anything to them about submitting a story for the Hemingway contest?"

George shook his head. "He didn't mention it, but apparently he wrote a lot and was always sending stuff to magazines hoping to get published."

Something troubled me, some needle of doubt that I couldn't articulate.

"What do you make of it?" George asked.

"I'm not sure."

"When you are, please let me know," George pleaded.

I nodded and turned back to the fight. The black kid was landing a series of combinations that rattled his opponent; the Hispanic's legs wobbled as he stood flat-footed on the canvas trying to dodge the next barrage of blows by ducking and grabbing on to the black kid's arms. Sweetwater separated them, looked into the Hispanic's eyes, then signaled for them to resume fighting. The black kid came in fast, feinted once, and came up inside the other's lowered hands, scoring a right to the chin that sent the kid in the designer trunks staggering backward to the ropes where he seemed to hang for a moment like a wounded bird caught in wire. Sweetwater gave him the mandatory standing eight count, then held the boy's face in his hands before ending the fight and helping the kid back to his corner, then going to raise the winner's hand to loud cheering from the audience. Sweets beamed.

"You seen Nick?" George asked, still standing beside me.

"I talked to him earlier." Sweetwater was getting out of the ring, taking a break between fights. I turned to leave.

"You see him, tell him I'm looking for him."

I nodded and began working my way through the crowd to the changing room where Sweetwater was headed.

I felt a tug on my jacket, turned, and saw Maggie behind me. "I thought you didn't care for this stuff."

"I don't," Maggie said, "I'm here because of Nick." She had frizzed her hair up and wore a hand-painted T-shirt and shorts. She looked younger.

"I talked to him earlier," I said.

"How did he seem?"

"Okay, why?" I wondered if Nick had said anything to her about the latest developments.

"He came over this evening and tried to talk me out of going to Vermont."

"I thought you'd discussed that a few months ago. He was agreeable."

"We'd talked about it, but Nick had never said how he felt one way or the other."

Something stirred again in me like a bad memory, one that had been too long repressed. "What changed his mind?" We were being pushed along in the crowd until I finally took Maggie's arm, found an opening, and escaped. I looked around and saw that we were standing by the pool house where only a few days ago Frank Maguire was found.

"More than anything I don't think he likes the idea of being so far away from Justin," Maggie said. "Especially at this age. I think he's afraid he'll lose contact with him. I was surprised. Nick doesn't usually express that kind of sentiment."

"You told me you knew about the notes he'd gotten recently?"

"Yes. Have there been more?"

"Yes, we may even have found a link in the second one to Frank Maguire's murder."

"Oh, God! Nick didn't say anything. But he seemed very depressed. I thought it was because of my decision. Is he in danger?"

"He could be."

Maggie put her hand on my arm. "Can you do anything?"

"I'm trying." A couple of drunks passed by; one of them stumbled, bumping into Maggie. She clutched my arm and I steadied her.

"I'm going to look for Nick," she said.

I nodded and watched her wend her way through the crowd. I wandered back to the changing room where Sweetwater sat on a bench, resting between fights. The next two fighters were dressed and shadowboxing around the room. I waved at Sweets and watched from outside the door, letting my thoughts spill around me like confetti. There was much to think about.

48.

The last two bouts went off without incident. By the time they were over, I could see that Sweetwater was as exhausted as the boxers. His step had slowed, but he still managed to control the fight, grinning as he raised each boy's hand before leaving the ring.

The crowd had grown rowdy and impossible to penetrate. I stayed on the fringe as much as possible, going over to congratulate Sweetwater when he left the ring. I told him I would walk home with him when he was ready. A couple of reporters, he said, wanted to talk to him, and then he was getting out of here. I looked at my watch. It was almost ten o'clock.

Jocelyn was coming out of Ruth Clampitt's office when I left Sweetwater. "Are you announcing the winners of the short-story contest?" I asked her.

"Yes. The second- and third-place contestants are here. I still haven't seen the winner."

"You won't. He's dead."

Jocelyn stared at me as if I'd related a bad joke. "What happened?"

I told her.

"What a tragedy."

I agreed. "Did you tell me how many judges read those stories?"

"Three."

"Was Nick one of them?"

"No." She named the two others besides herself. I didn't recognize the names of either of them.

"By the way," I said, "Wannamaker was still in college. Wouldn't it be unusual for a writer as young as Wannamaker was to write a story like 'Rain Delay'?"

"Because of his lack of experience, you mean?"

I nodded.

"Perhaps he was writing about his own childhood."

"Maybe, but I don't think so."

"Well, Hemingway wrote from experience, but it isn't the only method."

I saw Casey coming toward me as Jocelyn moved on.

"Bud," Casey said, "I want you to meet someone."

From behind Casey, clutching her hand, came a guy looking somewhat embarrassed. He had on shorts and a T-shirt, but something about the way he wore them told me he would probably have been more comfortable in a suit and tie.

"Bud, this is Mike."

We shook hands.

"Casey's talked a lot about you," Mike said.

"Nothing good." I smiled.

He seemed to be about Casey's age, with an open face, a quick, shy smile. Clean-cut and without obvious signs of any neurotic impulses, he appeared a perfect match for Casey. She looked at him with open affection. I was happy for her. Another mermaid singing, but not, as it turned out, for me.

"No," Mike said, "it's all been good."

"How is it going, Bud?" Casey asked. "Any developments?"

"A few, but don't expect any fireworks here tonight. Go off and have a good time." Mike and I shook hands again; Casey kissed me briefly on the lips, but I knew it represented the long good-bye. Another chapter closed. I watched sadly as they were swallowed up in the masses, then went on my way, skirting the crowd once more in search of Nick.

Jocelyn had taken the stage where Asia had been singing earlier. She was surrounded by Hemingway look-alikes as she announced the winners of the various contests that had been held all week, culminating in the announcement of the short-story winners, two of whom joined her on the stage; they were both women. She regretted, Jocelyn said, that the winner, Tim Wannamaker, author of "Rain Delay," was being awarded the prize posthumously. She related what had happened. There was silence, then scattered applause, but the crowd wanted entertainment, not an awards ceremony, and finally drifted away in search of refreshment.

Mickey Freeman sat on the front steps of the Hemingway House talking to Asia. I joined them. "Gideon," Asia said, "I was looking for you."

I glanced at Freeman, touching the still-tender knot on the back of my head. "Here I am."

"You know Mickey Freeman?"

"We've met." I didn't offer my hand.

"Mickey was just telling me about his latest venture."

"I'd like to hear about that. Does it involve some B and E?"

Freeman's expression became guarded. "What?"

"Breaking and entering," I said. "It's a felony around here. Coupled with assault and battery, it can change the way you spend your time."

Asia looked at Mickey.

"You're accusing me of what exactly?"

I looked him straight in the eye. "What about Maguire's notebooks that were on my desk?"

"What about them?"

"They aren't on my desk anymore."

"They aren't on mine either."

"I'm sorry to hear that, but the fact is they didn't belong on your desk."

"Well, I didn't take them. They turned up in the mail the other day."

"That's your story."

"It is and I'm sticking to it, pardner."

"I'm sure it will make interesting testimony in court. Who

did you say sent those notebooks to you?"

"I didn't. They came via an anonymous donor. And left the same way."

"Kind of interesting reading, wasn't it? Maybe even embarrassing now that Maguire's dead. Probably not the sort of thing you would like to see in the public eye."

Mickey grinned. "There was nothing incriminating there."

"Sure. And nothing to prove you benefited by Maguire's death, either."

"That's old ground, gumshoe. You've walked over it before."

Asia stood up. "Gideon, Mickey didn't kill Frank. Believe me."

"Why should I?"

"Because Mickey was with me from the time I left here that night until I got on the plane."

"Everybody needs somebody sometime," I said.

"It's true. I swear it," Asia said.

"I don't know true anymore." But truth be told, I did believe her, and Mickey Freeman. For all their posturing and power plays, they were harmless, I thought. "So what's the big venture?"

"Mickey's putting together a deal for a dinner theater along the harbor where I can sing whenever I'm in town. He's going to call it Asia's."

"Congratulations. Too bad Frank can't be here to witness your success."

They both ignored my sarcasm. My feelings weren't hurt. "I've found the cutest house, Gideon," Asia gushed, standing up and opening her arms. "I'll be here in the winter whenever I can get down." She stepped forward and put her arms around me. It was the night for damsel dismissals.

"Asia says you play a good piano," Mickey said.

"I have my nights."

"Maybe you could sit in once in a while."

"I've got a gig," I said, and turned and walked away.

Sweetwater was coming along the path from the back, and together we worked our way through the crowd to the front gate. Wallace had given up his sentinel post and we went out without incident. I accompanied Sweets to his home three blocks away, the smell of frangipani in the air. We didn't talk. He walked erect, his head high, but I could hear the shallow breathing and knew that the evening had taken its toll.

I told Sweets I'd see him for breakfast, then continued on uptown; with every step I took I could feel the heaviness of the night, weighted like an unwanted question.

49.

It was approaching midnight when I passed the courthouse and turned off Whitehead Street down Fleming, walking slowly as I measured out my steps, playing the recent conversations over in my head, and thinking, sometimes even catching myself as I muttered aloud.

I crossed Duval Street, which at this hour was still teeming with unfocused energy. At Simonton Street I stepped into a familiar residential neighborhood and sudden silence. Palm trees lined the sidewalks, their slender trunks almost white in the dim light, their fronds drooping. Three peaked roofs on houses that sat side by side established a rhythm as sweet and sad as a blues song carving into the night sky.

A lone car went by slowly, its headlights picking out the jagged edges of debris that lay in its path, and setting up a reflection, bouncing off the taillights of the cars parked along the one-way street, while music spilled softly from the moving car's interior.

It was here, within a block from here, that life began for me, and as I walked, I absorbed the sights and sounds as though it were yesterday, now with a sense of sudden awareness that it could also be the place where life would end. Crickets harmonized while invisible predators scurried beneath dry leaves. Still, at this hour the air was damp and my clothing clung to me, rivulets of sweat crawling on my body.

As I crossed William Street, the silence of the night was shattered briefly by a distant explosion. It could have been a car backfiring or a tire blowing; it could have been a firecracker. It could have been any number of things, but it wasn't. What it was, was a gunshot, a sound I'd heard often enough in my life, one that I'd heard too often in my mind, I thought, reaching for the Colt in my waistband as I broke into a sprint toward Nick Farr's apartment. I took the outside steps beside the bike shop two at a time. The screen door was ajar, the front door open, the interior apartment in darkness. "Nick!" I shouted. There was no answer.

I stepped inside, pointing the gun at the ceiling. I walked into the kitchen, the monotonous hum of the refrigerator's compressor the only sound. There were no lights. It smelled of dust and despair. The balcony was bathed in shadow, darkened by the canopy of trees that hid the night sky, but I could see that something, or someone, was slumped on the floor. I let out my breath and moved cautiously along the wall; a board creaked underfoot. I hesitated, checking the bedroom, which was empty, before stepping onto the balcony.

Nick was on the floor, on his back, his legs at an odd angle. He wore the same clothes he'd had when I last saw him a couple of hours earlier. I knelt down and took his outstretched wrist, searching for a pulse with the fingers of my left hand. It was weak, but he was alive. I leaned over him. He'd been shot in the chest; it looked like the scattershot made by a shotgun blast. A beer bottle was knocked over on the floor beside him, its freshly spilled contents seeping around Nick's body and the shotgun that lay nearby.

From the trees came the dizzying sound of cicadas. "Nick," I said close to his ear. I felt a movement as his hand reached for mine where I continued to hold his wrist. "It's me, Gideon."

He slowly licked his lips. "You were right," he said, his voice weak, barely a whisper.

"About what?"

"The notes."

"You wrote them yourself?"

Nick nodded.

"To get Maggie's sympathy?"

Another nod.

"And the story, too."

Nick nodded once.

"Why the notes, Nick? And why try to finger Wanna-maker?"

"You think... I killed Maguire." Nick's eyes closed.

Yes, I had thought so. I didn't remember when I had worked it out, but it had been in the back of my mind, simmering; maybe when I saw Maggie at the party tonight, I also saw the possibility that Nick could have used those notes, first to gain Maggie's sympathy, and then, after Maguire was killed, to shield himself from blame by making it look as if some psycho was out there who had it in for writers, particularly pretenders to the Hemingway throne. He had watched every angle of the investigation knowing when it was time to move. I had even told him that the Sweetwater decoy was a ruse so he didn't have to worry about him. The motive had bothered me, but I suppose on the way over here I'd worked that out, too. Nick's career was crumbling, his personal life in a shambles. Jocelyn wasn't happy with Maguire, so Nick had played up to her. Once Maguire was gone, Nick would have been the obvious next in line.

"I'm going to call an ambulance." I started to get up. His hand gripped a little tighter.

There was a brief rustle in the trees, a cooling breeze that swept across the balcony. Nick's head moved slightly. "Wall," he whispered. "Man alone... ain't got no..." He was sweating, working. "...walls." Nick shut his eyes and lay there.

I freed my hand from his and held it over his heart, which was still beating. Then I stood up and went to the phone and called for help.

50.

The sound of a siren cut through the heat and stillness of the night. I tucked my gun back in the waistband of my pants and went into the bathroom, where I washed the blood from my hands and scooped cool water from the faucet onto my face. The squeal of the siren intensified, then died on the street out front. I stepped out on the porch and watched two paramedics carry up the stretcher, then showed them where Nick was. They were getting him on the gurney when a couple of cops I knew arrived. I told them what had happened without relating any of what Nick had said. Then I followed the medics down to the ambulance with Nick.

"What are his chances?" I asked.

"Can't tell you that," one of them said, getting in the back with Nick. "We'll do our best."

I watched them speed off, the siren blaring, before walking back to the stairway leading up to Nick's apartment. Standing at the foot of the stairs, it was impossible to look up the street. Someone could have run down from Nick's, then turned back and along a path that ran to the rear of the building. Because the stairs were set back from the sidewalk, I would not have seen whomever it was as I was walking here. I followed a path to where it joined a lane that gave onto William Street, a perfect escape route.

When I returned, George Lewis was standing at the foot of the stairs talking to one of the two cops who'd arrived earlier.

"What the hell are you doing?" George demanded.

"I was on my way over here to talk to Nick when I heard a

shot. I ran up there and found him on the balcony."

The cop lit a cigarette, his face briefly illuminated in the flame from his lighter.

"You were paying a social call at this time of night?"

"I had a couple of questions for him."

"Must have been important, they couldn't wait till morning. Did he answer them?"

I nodded. "Nick didn't kill Frank Maguire."

"Who did, then?"

"The same person who tried to kill Nick."

"And who might that be?"

"I'm working on it."

George studied me woodenly. Finally he shook his head and said, "Get out of here, Sherlock, but don't go so far I can't find you first thing in the morning."

I watched them mount the stairs to Nick's apartment before I walked back up Fleming. Turning onto William Street, I crept along the darkened, quiet sidewalk until I reached Maggie's. The lights were out. It was after one o'clock in the morning. I climbed the steps to the porch and knocked lightly. Then again a little louder. A light came on. Someone came to the door. Maggie's voice said, "Who is it?"

"Gideon."

The door opened and Maggie looked at me and raised a hand to her face. "It's okay. I need to come in."

Maggie unlatched the screen door and pushed it open, holding it for me as I went in. She closed the door. I stood in the center of the room.

"Maggie, Nick's been shot. He's at the hospital."

"What happened?" She gripped the folds of her robe in one hand and pressed the other hand against her face and sobbed.

"At first I thought he'd tried to kill himself. Now I'm not so sure."

I let her cry, and when she had regained some control, I filled her in as best I could.

"Nick? You thought Nick killed Frank Maguire? Why?"

"I went over there to ask him about it," I said without going into details. "I got there just after he was shot. He told me he knew I thought he'd killed Frank."

Maggie bowed her head. I waited. "Did he say anything else?"

"He wasn't making much sense."

"Tell me."

I repeated Nick's jumbled words as best I could remember them. A tortured smile creased Maggie's lips. "Oh, that was Hemingway. God, everything down here is Hemingway."

"What?"

"Hemingway. Nick was always saying it. It was from one of the novels." She walked over to a bookcase, found a book, and brought it to me. *To Have and Have Not.* Hemingway's Key West novel. Maggie thumbed through it. "Harry Morgan. That's the character who says it when he's dying." She found the passage and handed the book to me. "'A man alone ain't got no chance.'"

I read Harry Morgan's dying words. "Nick said 'walls.' A man alone ain't got no walls."

Maggie shook her head. "Walls. It doesn't make any sense."

From upstairs Justin called, "Mommy, who's there?"

"Go back to sleep," Maggie said, crying softly again.

"Maybe it does."

"What?"

"Make sense." I wanted to go. "Maggie, do you want to go to the hospital?"

"I can't leave Justin."

"Take him. He can sleep there and you can be with Nick."

"Oh, God, yes, I want to be there."

"Do you want me to call a cab?"

"No, I'll drive. What are you going to do?"

"Go find the person who killed Frank and shot Nick."

51.

I stood beneath the twisted branches of a mahogany tree staring up at the gingerbread men that decorated the second-story porch railing. From the sidewalk the windows in the house were dark.

Walls. Wallace.

It was a name Nick Farr had given me. Mixed up with a soliloquy from a dying character provided by a dead writer whose work Nick had inherited. I quietly climbed the dusty stairs to Wallace's apartment door, taking out the Colt that was my inheritance. I stood outside the door, the Colt hanging loosely from my hand, listening. There was no sound from inside the apartment. I stood along the wall and tried the door. It was open. I waited, listening, but inside there was a deadly dream-like silence.

I went in, keeping my back to the wall, and with my free hand searched for a light switch. I found it and flipped on the light. A ceiling light came on and lit the room. No bodies were on the floor, or anywhere else. I eased toward the back of the shotgun apartment, keeping clear of the doorway to Wallace's bedroom, which was just beyond the kitchen. I found the light switch there and turned on another light in another empty room. The bedroom, too, was uninhabited, the bed still made up. I checked the bathroom. Wallace wasn't home.

I turned the lights off and left, walking back out into the scented night, along the old streets with their rippled sidewalks, full of silent memory. A full moon was making its early descent across the western sky as I approached the Hemingway House.

The grounds were quiet; the only evidence of the recent party lay in bits of scattered debris that could be seen here and there in the foliage and along the porch. The house was dark, the iron gate to the entrance, locked. I looked up and down the empty street before boosting myself over the brick wall that surrounded the estate.

Walking across the sidewalk, I climbed the steps to the porch where an empty plastic cup skittered in the wake of my march across the porch, making a hollow sound against the stillness. I tried the front door; it was locked. I went back down the sidewalk and followed it around the side yard to the boxing ring, where I stood motionless, the same place I'd stood earlier in the evening, in the shadows, staring at the buildings in back of the house, all swathed in darkness except for a dim light that showed in the window of Hemingway's writing studio. Cats prowled around my ankles. I waited several minutes, then climbed the outside steps to the studio.

From the landing I could not see in the window. I knocked on the door. "Wallace, it's Gideon Lowry." From inside I heard a subtle shifting, the rustle of movement, before the light leaking from the window was suddenly extinguished. I couldn't remember ever being in the studio and didn't know if there was another way out.

I took the Colt from my waistband and tested the door, which was open. The studio interior was in total darkness, while enough light reflected from the street and the night sky to create shadows around the landing where I stood. I kept a shoulder pressed to the brick wall away from the doorway.

"Nick Farr was shot tonight," I said, and waited.

Finally, Wallace's thin voice said, "What's that got to do with me? Every time somebody's shot in this town am I going to have you at my door?"

"Whose door?"

"I was cleaning up. I came up here to rest and fell asleep."

"Why'd you turn the light off?"

"I heard something. I didn't know who was out there."

"So turn it back on."

"I like the dark."

"Look, Nick is alive. He wasn't killed. I got to him just after he was shot."

"What's that got to do with me?" Wallace spoke barely above a whisper now as though others could hear us.

"Nick was in the house the other night when Frank Maguire was shot, wasn't he? He told you about Maguire's plans for moving in once Mickey Freeman bought the place. You were going to be out more than just a job. This house is your life and you were being put out to pasture. Nick told you about Frank, what he was working on. You just look like Hemingway, Frank was actually writing him. Later, you saw an opportunity to ingratiate yourself with Mickey Freeman by breaking into my office, stealing Frank's notebooks, and giving them to Freeman."

"You can prove all of that?"

"Do I have to? Nick's alive, Wallace. He named you."

"I don't believe you."

"Pick up the phone and call the hospital."

"I've been here all night."

"You weren't at your post when I left, which wasn't long before Nick was shot."

"What does that prove?"

"Nick Farr was your only obstacle. He didn't actually see you kill Maguire, but he must have known you were around then. And he also knew that he was going to be a major suspect if it came out that he was in the house. You thought you were protected, but you couldn't be sure, especially after you'd seen me talking to him and Mickey Freeman tonight. Was Nick expecting you tonight? Did he tell you to come over after the party, or was it a surprise visit?"

"It's late and I'm tired. Leave me alone."

"No. It's over now. Come out, Wallace."

There was another long silence, then I heard a chair scrape across the floor, and Wallace's heavy tread. I raised the Colt. He stepped out on the landing, his bearded face dejected looking, his eyes squinting at me as if he didn't recognize me. His hands were empty. I lowered the Colt.

"What are you going to do?" Wallace asked.

"Take you down to talk to George Lewis. He's over at Nick Farr's place right now."

"I've got nothing to say to him."

"Let's let George be the judge of that. Come on." I motioned for Wallace to go ahead of me.

Wallace closed the door to the studio, then started down the stairs. I kept the Colt hanging loose in my hand. The iron stairway shivered slightly under our combined weight. When we got to the bottom, Wallace hesitated. "I've got to turn off the pool light," he said. I looked across the side yard to the pool, its underwater light casting a ghostly white reflection, the old rectangular pool where, as a kid, I'd once gone swimming. I followed Wallace to the pool house. He opened the door and stepped just inside and flipped a switch. The pool light went out.

Wallace emerged from the pool house and I saw the gun too late. Something small, barely visible in the palm of his large hand. The gun coughed once, spitting a brief flame in my direction, as Wallace turned and ran. I felt heat, as if I'd been stung, on the upper part of my left arm. Wallace was moving toward the swimming pool, moving fast for a man his age, I thought. "Stop!" I shouted. Wallace turned and fired once again as I went down on one knee, raising the Colt. My hand shook as I squeezed the trigger, hearing the roar, that noise that I dreaded, the last sound my father and brother ever heard.

Then I heard the splash as Wallace hit the water. I walked to the pool. He was floating there, facedown near the side. I tucked the Colt away, then reached in with my good hand and grabbed him by the back of the shirt, hauling him over the side until his upper body at least was out of the water. He was breathing, coughing up water. I looked at my left arm where the fabric of the sport coat was torn and bloody.

A neighbor must have heard the gunshot and called the police. I sat down on the ground and listened for the second time that night as a siren rent the still night air.

52.

It was superficial, a flesh wound, one that would leave only a minor scar. The following night I was back at the piano in the Pier House. During a break Ronnie asked me some questions about the case, which I conveniently sidestepped. The papers would provide the details the next day, I told her. And I was right.

Wallace's journal, or at least the portion of it that was found in the Hemingway writing studio, was published in the *Miami Herald*. It was a meandering account of his lifelong effort to write, to emulate the master whose house Wallace had appropriated for himself. The journal, of course, was more than a record of failure; it also provided a portrait of a twisted personality, a document that would, the paper suggested, be used as evidence in the trial to prosecute Wallace for the murder of Frank Maguire and the attempted murder of Nick Farr. But Wallace had achieved his fifteen minutes of fame, and the pictures of him being taken into custody when he was released from the hospital showed a man who appeared serene and confident. He had shaved his beard; without it the resemblance to Hemingway was fleeting. In a sense, I thought, Wallace had discovered his own identity.

Nick Farr would recover. I don't know when I figured out that it was Nick who had written the short story "Rain Delay," but it had been lurking in the back of my mind, I suppose, ever since Maggie told me about Nick's objections to her plans to take Justin and move back to Vermont, a sort of parallel to the story that Jocelyn had described to me. I also learned later that

Nick had written the story in an attempt to relieve some of the anguish he was feeling over the possible loss of Maggie and Justin. Once he heard about Wannamaker's death, Nick decided to enter it in the contest which would allow him to take a kind of macabre pleasure in its authorship if the story won.

Once Maguire was killed, Nick was able to use Wannamaker as a way of diverting attention from himself. I had begun to see Nick as a possible suspect in Maguire's murder; he had, of course, much to gain from Frank's death. But, instead, he was simply a manipulator, using the notes he was writing and sending to himself in an effort to win back Maggie, who had grown weary of his philandering. In a way, he had been successful. Maggie called to tell me that they were going to try to reconcile once Nick got out of the hospital. She sounded better than I'd heard her in a long time. I wished them both success while privately feeling that Maggie was giving in, a sort of emotional alcoholic, and that Nick would never change.

Key West's literary community had seen to that. With so much competition among them for the Hemingway legacy, they had insured that there would always be a hard scramble for the prize, constantly giving rise to men like Nick Farr. As I saw it, they had become just another user group that would ultimately burden my already overburdened hometown.

Asia, of course, was jet-setting around the country promoting her latest recording, a selection of old torch songs. I bought the tape and found, to my amusement, a recording of "Night and Day," which contained, in small print on the back, a dedi - cation to Gideon Lowry.

The state of Florida shot down hope for renewal of the offshore oil leases in our waters—at least for the upcoming year. And after a blistering profile appeared in *Rolling Stone,* under Dan Riggs's byline, Mickey Freeman announced that he was turning his attention to the entertainment industry.

As for me, I still play a weekend gig in one bar or another

in Key West, while working around the house and office by day. Weeknights I can be found at my desk, usually with the company of a cat, the poetry of T. S. Eliot, and the measured ticking of the pendulum clock keeping me in touch with the past. The Colt .45 remains out of sight in a drawer, but never for long out of mind.

The End

The Gideon Lowry Mysteries

Killing Me Softly
Night and Day
Love for Sale
Blue Moon

Also by John Leslie

Border Crossing (2013)

and

The Florida Mysteries

Blood on the Keys
Bounty Hunter Blues
Killer in Paradise
Damaged Goods
Havana Hustle

CPSIA information can be obtained
at www.ICGtesting.com
Printed in the USA
LVHW080020120722
723264LV00032B/1178